EVERY DAY

is Christmas

BY

PAT SIMMONS

Developmental Editor: Chandra Sparks Splond
Proofread by Judicious Revisions LLC; Miriam "Cookie" Mitchell
Beta Reader: Evangelist Charlotte Townsend
Interior Design: Kimolisa/Fiverr.com
Cover Design: designerboard18/fiverr.com

Praise for Pat Simmons

I love *Couple by Christmas*. It was a wonderful Christmas story and such a beautiful testament to the spirit and presence of God for what and how He can bring a marriage back together, what God has joined together let no man put asunder; I will definitely share this book with family and friends and others looking for a good Christmas book, and a good Christian love story. This was a wonderful read. I love the Author she's just the greatest♡—Mary

Waiting for Christmas. This book is amazing, I actually enjoyed my time reading this book. Pat Simmons is the Queen of clean and Godly stories. I Love it!!!! Ciara has a heart to give. Sterling and Ciara make a great couple although they have their own issues. It was awesome to see how their relationship blossoms into something Beautiful. God, as always, is the reason for every season. Pat Simmons, may God Bless your creative hand as always. 🙌♥🙏☺ Rubykat

Christmas Takeover was a sweet family story that gives you a glimpse into how Christmas should be celebrated Jamieson-style. Pat Simmons weaved a story filled with fun, humor, love, and change. Pace and Harmony will warm your heart with each look and conversation centered around the meaning of Christmas… Enjoyable, fast-paced read.—Msmagnolia Reads

EVERY DAY
is Christmas

Chapter One

Of all the times for Gina Christmas's father, Ray, to be under the weather, tax season was forbidden.

How could their family-owned accounting firm, Christmas Tax Help for All Seasons, run without him? Her father was convalescing from back surgery until the third week of April.

I can do this. I can fly solo for the next six weeks until April 15. Sure I can.

Although Gina was a proficient certified public accountant, she had serious reservations about meeting the April 15 deadline for all their clients. Between completing upcoming quarterly reports for the company's clients and filing tax returns for repeat customers, she was swamped. However, she couldn't fail her father or herself.

The company started as a small storefront shop, which had been expanded and upgraded twice in the past fifteen years. It was the brainchild of Gina's grandfather, George, who was good with numbers despite lacking a formal education and had a kind demeanor. Grandpa called it living up to his Christmas surname. Plus, he always credited his parents for instilling in him a responsibility to live for Christ daily to please God. That sentiment was passed down to Gina's dad, then to Gina and her two siblings, Denise and John, the oldest. George currently enjoyed retirement in Arizona.

Gina's stomach growled as she reviewed the Missouri state and federal tax returns with Mr. Thomas in her father's office. The client had been a widower for two years now, and he liked keeping his children close, which was the source of his complaints while she prepared his taxes.

The door chimed in the lobby, alerting Gina that the next customer had arrived forty minutes early.

"Have a seat. I'll be with you in a moment," she shouted.

To keep the paperwork orderly, Gina met with her clients across the hall in her office. Gina had been so busy she hadn't bothered to open the blinds in their separate offices, which gave them a full view of the spacious lobby decorated with five plants—Gina's limit to water— warm beige walls, cobalt blue trendy furniture with pops of burgundy accents, and a fully stocked snack bar in a corner nook. The snacks were reasonably priced, and all the proceeds went directly to one of two charities—the Round-Up program, where change added up when round to the nearest dollar, and Every Day is Christmas.

Even though Gina tried to space out the appointments by two hours—a challenging task when combining her clients and her father's—she was still overextended.

Gina resumed explaining to Mr. Thomas why his refund wouldn't be as generous as the previous year.

"Robin worked last year, so you can't claim her as a dependent on your taxes. You could on your previous tax season because she was unemployed."

"She still eats and sleeps at our house." Mr. Thomas rubbed his premature gray hair. He frowned at the amount.

"I found every deduction I could, but your adult children working is good. They can help with household expenses, and that will take some of the burden off you." Gina couldn't sympathize with the father of three. His "children" were well-educated but picky about job offers and turned them down for frivolous reasons. Now, inching close to their thirties, they had excuses on standby for not moving out.

"I know you did, Miss Christmas." He nodded. "You're better at finding stuff than your father." He leaned closer and chuckled. "Don't tell Ray I said that."

Gina smiled. The client's compliment would make her father proud. She followed in his footsteps and earned her accounting degree from Harris-Stowe State University, one of two of Missouri's historically black colleges and universities. She passed the Uniformed CPA Examination and continued with more classes until she fulfilled every requirement to obtain her license.

"Here." She pointed to the lines she had marked. "If you sign these forms, I can e-file them to Jeff City for your state and Kansas City for your federal returns. Consider making more charitable contributions before next year's tax season. You can also increase your contributions to your company's 401(k) and IRA account."

Clients knew Gina had founded a nonprofit, Every Day is Christmas, and was on its board of directors. Although it was against the code of ethics to even hint at making a donation to the charity, this charity helped nurture creativity for youth in a children's home.

"I never turn down the opportunity to give," Mr. Thomas said, although he wasn't happy about his refund amount.

"I know you don't, and God blesses us when we bless others." Gina got up and walked the client out of the office. Entering the lobby, she froze at the sight of the next client. Gina steadied herself against the wall to catch her breath.

She inhaled, and a new faint scent tickled her nose. It wasn't the vanilla and rosemary air freshener from the plug-in by the window. Suddenly, the office's stylish decor faded in the background as the man became the accent piece. He stood from his relaxing pose in one of four club chairs to greet her.

Tall and built like a warrior.

His eyebrows, trimmed mustache, and jet-black beard complemented his flawless medium-brown skin. Gina wanted to cry because the man's handsomeness was blinding. *Wow*.

Judging from his crisp jade Oxford shirt and creased black slacks, he worked in an office. A slight smile tugged on his full lips when he made eye contact with her. There was a mix of confusion and attraction…maybe.

"Hi. Do you have an appointment?"

"No," he stated. His baritone voice rang in her ears, sealing whatever deal he placed on the table, including pro bono for his taxes.

This couldn't be real. He was too priceless not to have bodyguards to protect his assets.

He took one step forward. "I don't have an appointment."

No! She wanted to scream. Disappointment made her heart sink that she wouldn't get to learn more about him, but relief flooded her senses because there was no wiggle room for a new client. "Sorry, I'm swamped, and my dad's out. I can't take any walk-ins." Gina remained professional despite suffering from star-struck-itis.

He didn't hide his confusion. "Isn't this a Christmas store?"

Gina smiled. "Sorry, no, although we showcase Christian Christmas–themed ornaments. It's March fifteen—too early for Christmas items."

Squinting, the unnamed man studied her. "Your sign says Christmas for All Seasons."

She giggled and stretched out her hand at the handsome stranger. "I'm Gina Christmas, and it's Christmas Tax Help for All Seasons, our family accounting business."

He turned away from her and laughed to himself, then faced her again. "I feel stupid. My grandmother told me months ago there was a year-round Christmas shop downtown that sold unique Christian Christmas–themed items. Then she was in the hospital, and out of the blue, she asked me about it this morning and was insistent that it wasn't too late to get her a one-of-a-kind ornament. So I took a chance and came downtown looking for a Christmas shop." His embarrassment peeked through his good looks as he accepted her hand. "I'm Landon Michaels."

"Ah, someone liked Westerns." She couldn't resist the twist on the name of actor Michael Landon, who had played Little Joe Cartwright on *Bonanza*.

"Usually, seniors get the name recognition. Most people in our generation don't know of Michael Landon."

"You're right. I'm thirty-two, but I've watched plenty of reruns with my grandfather."

His eyes seemed to glow as he nodded. "My grandmother loved *Highway to Heaven* and *Little House on the Prairie*. She thought it was the perfect name for me." His smile was filled with adoration. "She's the same one who sent me on this expedition out of season."

He had a sense of humor and loved his grandparents—a plus.

"I've never met anyone with the last name Christmas." He snickered and folded his arms as if he were in no hurry while Gina had to get ready for her next client.

"I'm glad to be the first, and I get that a lot. I'm thankful my parents didn't name my sister or me Mary, Holly, or any other seasonal names. Speaking of seasons, we allow a charity to display their Christmas-themed gifts crafted by young artisans from low-income homes and shelters, mostly the children's home. Some inventory comes in for Christmas in July, but October begins the Christmas season."

"So this is the right place." Slipping his hands into his pockets, he seemed to look at her through the hood of thick black lashes.

Gina had to depend on top-brand mascara for that effect. "Sort of. You can go online for more information about the charity's history, little artisans, and past masterpieces."

She beamed with Godly pride for the children. "But…if you are hungry, we stock our nook with snacks, and you can round up your purchase to the nearest dollar to give to the same charity." The door chimed, and her father's next clients walked inside.

She smiled at Mr. and Mrs. Jackson. "I'll be with you in a minute," she greeted, then faced Landon again. "Sorry. I don't have what you're looking for, but perhaps a snack?"

The nook was the brainchild of Gina and her sister, Denise, when they were small and tagged along to work with their dad and grandfather. They stocked it with goodies purchased with their allowance money and were able to keep the proceeds. As they became older and got jobs, they continued with their snack bar but donated the proceeds to charities. Their customers were clients, neighboring merchants, and delivery persons who purchased chips, cookies, candy, nutritional bars, or drinks like bottled water, juice, and soda.

His lips twitched, almost in irritation. "Not interested. Thank you for your time. I'll let my grandmother know you're out of stock." He turned and left with his cologne trailing him.

When the door closed, Gina stuck out her tongue.

The Jacksons shook their heads, and Mr. Jackson grunted. "What's a dollar or two to give back and help others? His attitude is part of the problem with young people today."

Mrs. Jackson *tsk*ed.

Gina couldn't agree more. The man had irresistible looks and a friendly personality but lacked a cheerful giver mentality. If he had a girlfriend, he would probably have her pay whenever they went out.

Having wasted enough time she couldn't retrieve, Gina waved the Jacksons back to her dad's office.

The joke was on Landon. How was he supposed to know that many of the angel ornaments and decorations his grandmother owned had been purchased from an accounting company, not a Christmas store?

What a wasted trip. As Landon had walked into the lobby and looked around, he realized nothing resembled a retail store. The interior was a stylish commercial business. A corner nook reminded him of a hotel ministore where guests could buy toiletries or snacks. Child-inspired handmade signs encouraged people to buy from their little store. There were bags of peanuts, chips, cookies, and other snacks.

He had skipped lunch to drive fifteen minutes from his Clayton office to downtown St. Louis, but it wasn't worth it, and he was about to leave when the stunning Gina Christmas appeared.

Landon almost forgot his name, feeling like a shy schoolboy instead of a thirty-five-year-old civil engineer.

His rush back to the office no longer mattered. He liked being in her company until she mentioned donating. He checked out mentally. There had to be a phobia about giving away money to supposedly help others because Landon had an illness that seemed to suffocate him.

He huffed as he steered his vehicle back to his office. Granny Lonna would be disappointed when he told her the visit had been a bust.

His grandmother's health was deteriorating due to dreaded dementia. Time was not on her side, nor their family's. Whatever Granny Lonna wanted, she got, except maybe this time. Landon would look somewhere else. Would she enjoy Christmas this year if she didn't know who she was?

Stopping at a light, Landon frowned, wondering if his grandmother's mind was already on the decline because she was adamant that the business sold ornaments year-round.

He called her through his Bluetooth.

"Landon, my favorite grandson," she answered cheerfully. "Were you able to find the Christmas store?" Worry lined her voice.

Had she already forgotten Landon was her only grandson out of five grandchildren? "No, Granny Lonna. The place was a tax service, and the woman said they would probably have some things come in July or, at the latest, October. It's just an odd setup. I thought it was a year-round Christmas shop."

Landon got it; it was a seasonal side hustle. He did spy a large box peeping from behind a sofa marked *Every Day is Christmas*, stuffed with strings of lights and tree toppers. There was no telling what else was behind the furnishings.

"Well, they have one-of-a-kind pieces, so please check back—regularly," his grandmother urged. "Like every month. In a couple of weeks sounds even better."

Granny Lonna wouldn't take no for an answer. Landon conceded, and the cheerfulness returned to her voice.

"Yes, Ma'am."

"That's my grandson. Now, pick the most beautiful Black angel for me."

"Okay." The two chatted for a few more minutes until Landon heard the doorbell ring, and then, seconds later, Judy Miller's voice, the nursing aide from the senior living community who came to do her daily health check.

Before ending the call, he asked to speak with Judy to ensure his grandmother's vitals and appetite were good.

Tugging on the strands of his mustache, Landon thought about how he would spend his lunch. He would grab a sandwich from the café in the building. Then his thoughts switched back to Gina Christmas. At first sight, the woman was gorgeous, and his assessment improved each moment they talked. Landon would have fallen on the floor if he hadn't been sitting.

She was beautiful and commanding. Friendly, confident, and…dare he say, a gold digger?

What woman asks a stranger for money?

Those in need, God whispered.

He paused his internal tirade. God knew he wasn't stingy with his money, but Landon liked to follow the trail to see where his money stopped. Had his grandmother known the place was a front for a charity? What kind of charity? To benefit who, with what, and when? Sometimes, people were too generous with their money and failed to ask questions.

How often had he donated to causes and later learned that they didn't receive the services or money as promised? Landon hadn't entirely closed the door when he heard her mumble, "Not a cheerful giver. The nerve of that woman. She didn't know him.

Instead of giving cash, Landon's charity was volunteering, spending one-on-one time with folks, and seeing what they needed with his own eyes.

My eyes see everything—good and evil, God whispered. *I judge the heart, including yours.*

Landon prayed that he wouldn't judge, and it was hard when dishonest people walked among them. He preferred doing.

In fact, he had invited a teenage neighbor who lived with his grandmother to a professional soccer match between opposing teams, St. Louis City SC and D.C. United, at City Park downtown, near the Christmas store next weekend. When Landon learned the boy would rather watch, play, and breathe the game, forsaking his academics, Landon knew he had to do something.

Bradley Nelson needed quality time, not a handout without a father in the home, much like the homeless man who needed food for nourishment.

Landon cared less about soccer. He was a Kansas City Chiefs fan and had driven three and a half hours across the state to watch an NFL game.

Take that, Miss Merry Christmas, he thought in his defense when Gina's pretty face, which looked soft to the touch, popped into his mind. Landon dismissed the attraction and focused on his mentee. With the cost of the seats, snacks at the game, plus a light dinner before, the price tag on his outing with Bradley was hundreds of dollars.

Gina Christmas knew nothing about Landon's character.

"She is one of My disciples, working to help others," God whispered, *"as are you. Study My Word in Matthew twenty-five, verses thirty-five to forty, and you will see all those who work in My harvest don't have the same duties."*

Landon parked in his assigned garage parking spot and walked toward the elevator, pondering what God had said. He shrugged. "Okay, Lord, I won't judge her. I hope You took her to task for judging me."

That's petty.

Since Granny Lonna's dementia was advancing, Landon planned to act cordially the next time he stopped at Christmas Tax Help for All Seasons. He would visit again and again until a Black angel piece arrived. Then, Landon would buy it and hope it wouldn't be too late for his grandmother to enjoy Christmas, whatever day it was.

"Look out, Miss Christmas, I'm about to become a thorn in your shapely little side."

Chapter Two

Working fifty-plus hours during tax season wasn't the norm, but it was Gina's reality without her father in the office. Although her demanding workload didn't leave Gina much room for entertainment, nothing would stop her from attending the production of *The Little Mermaid* at the Fox Theatre. Nothing.

Not only were they good seats, but they were free—one of the perks of having an older sister who worked in television sales. The downside was Denise was a homebody after work and had no problem giving those tickets away.

Gina was the opposite. She worked diligently in the office, and once five o'clock hit, she was ready to explore events around town. Her father usually walked out the door with her. That was before Dad's surgery.

Now Fred, a mail carrier who lived in one of the adjacent loft apartments, showed up as the sun set to walk her safely to her car, despite her protests. "Mr. Christmas would expect this of us."

What could Gina say but thank you, and never decline an act of kindness again.

"Would you hurry up?" Denise demanded. "You said you would treat me to dinner since I have the tickets." She stood in the doorway of Gina's bedroom with her arms crossed. Dress up to Denise was jewelry she'd forgo during the week and curls, a hairstyle that was too troublesome during the week.

"I have the fixings for a quick salad in the fridge." Gina was half serious. This was the last show, and Gina would put on as much makeup as needed to look refreshed and drink however many cups of coffee to stay alert to relive the remake of the childhood story.

Denise shook her head. "Oh no, you're not skimping on my meal. Now hurry up." Her stomach growled.

People often said they could pass as twins. Denise was four years older, inches taller than Gina's five-foot-six, and ten pounds heavier. The sisters didn't live far away from each other. Both were single and educated. According to their parents, they were attractive, too.

"Hold on." Gina studied her reflection in the mirror. Sleeping late this Saturday morning didn't erase the darkness under her eyes, which she had accumulated from staying up until three to work on taxes.

"Thirty days and tax season will be over." Gina sighed as she dabbed more concealer under her brown eyes to make her best asset pop.

"Ooh, I need to get you my tax stuff. You still look tired," Denise said without Gina asking her opinion. "You know, we could have donated the tickets."

"You're joking, right? Because I've been waiting for this." Gina tried to keep a steady hand as she applied mascara. "*The Little Mermaid* was our favorite movie growing up. Remember when Mom and Dad tried bribing us with treats or a new toy? Too late, we were hooked. John threatened to run away from home if we kept rewinding the singing scene."

The sisters laughed, recalling their older brother's antics to keep them from re-watching the movie, like hiding the tape or bribing them with his allowance to do something else. Payback came when they were grown; John met his wife, Terri, who was a *Little Mermaid* fan too. It's too bad the couple lived in Chicago, where they were both successful attorneys.

"Personally, I don't know where you're getting all this energy to go to a matinée."

Gina chuckled. "It's called coffee. And don't forget about *Shen Yun* in a few weeks."

Denise groaned. "You're aging me, sis, dragging me to movies and outings on the weekends. You need a husband to accompany you to these places."

"I have no prospects until he comes along, so you'll have to be my escort, best friend, and sister." She admired her handiwork, then stood from her vanity table.

"Gina, come on. I'm hungry." Denise pouted.

Minutes later, Gina slid into the passenger seat of Denise's car, trying to stifle a yawn while her sister drove to Midtown, about twenty minutes away. Yes, Gina was tired, but her profession paid the bills and added to her savings while leaving her personal life deficient.

"Yikes, girl. Can you look at this traffic?" Gina mumbled.

Denise sighed. "There must be some other event going on, too."

A sea of red, blue, and yellow fans headed east on Washington Avenue. "Looks like a soccer game."

"Good thing we made reservations at The Club to eat before the show."

Ten minutes and five blocks later, the sisters located a free parking spot since the garages were filled.

"It's good we're accustomed to stepping in heels, and the weather is nice," Denise said.

"Yep." But Gina's feet would pay the price for looking cute when she returned to the car.

Once inside the restaurant, they approached the desk to give their names.

"One moment," the woman, who reminded Gina of a college student with her twin braids and cheerful personality, said.

"Thank you," Gina and Denise replied in unison as they twirled to have a seat.

Suddenly, the double doors to the restaurant seemed to open automatically, and Landon Michaels walked in with a confident swagger.

Although it didn't look like he was trying to garner attention, he was too late. There was something about a man who carried himself like a prince, looked camera-ready like a model, and didn't know how much power he had over any woman with eyes, with or without contacts. The man was just as handsome in casual attire as he was days ago in her office.

"Humph," Denise said as Landon's eyes rested on Gina.

"Miss Christmas?" His voice was as strong as his features when he approached her before speaking with the hostess.

"Mr. Michaels," she said, looking up. He towered over her by at least four to five inches.

"Call me Landon," he said.

"Christmas," the hostess called out.

Heads turned as if the name was a code word for fire or another disaster.

A bystander nearby chuckled. "Christmas. That's nine months away," he said.

"Here." The sisters raised their hands.

That's what Gina disliked most about her surname. There was always someone who had a joke to make. She and Denise followed the hostess to their table.

"Your server will be right with you." The woman smiled, placed the plastic tan menus before them, and left.

Denise didn't pick hers up. Instead, she drummed her fingers on the table. "Who's Landon?"

Gina looked up and shrugged. "Just a rude man who had an attitude when he came into the office looking for any leftover Christmas decorations."

"Yeah, we usually sell the last pieces by the end of January." Denise snickered, tilted her head, and squinted. "He didn't seem rude to *me* just now. All I saw was his eyes dancing when he saw you. And you seemed just as affected. Why am I sitting here with you when someone else could take you to a play?"

"Did you not hear what I said? We're not friends or enemies. We know very little about one another."

"Which could be resolved on or before the first date." Denise smiled.

Gina grunted at her sister's nonsense. She picked up her menu and perused her choices. Their server appeared minutes later, and they placed their order.

"Where is your ladies' room?" Denise asked the server, then excused herself.

While waiting, Gina glanced around the restaurant. The place was packed with families and couples. She was thankful for her sister, who got these amazing tickets. Otherwise, Gina would miss out because they were pricey for her girlfriends to want to go with her.

Gina took her phone out of her purse and scrolled through the notifications. Their food arrived minutes before Denise returned, and Gina was about to investigate. "Girl, are you okay?"

"Yep." She had a suspicious sparkle in her eyes. "I stopped to chat. Great. Our food is here." She slid into the booth, said grace, and began to sample her beef brisket.

"With whom?" Frowning, Gina craned her neck to look for a recognizable face. She didn't see anyone she knew, and Denise didn't tell her.

Soon, they finished and asked for their check. As they were leaving, Gina spied Landon and a teenager at a table engaged in a conversation that had them both laughing.

Not only did the man have a nice smile, but the sound of his laugh was distinct, even though the buzz of the guests. That was strange because she had only met him once, so why did Gina feel this odd connection?

They didn't even like each other, did they?

Landon's teenage neighbor, Bradley, had his full attention until a woman approached their table.

"Pardon me," she said. "You don't know me."

"No, I don't." Landon squinted and noticed a strong resemblance to Gina Christmas before she invited herself to the empty chair at their table.

"My name is Denise Christmas, Gina's older sister."

That explained their similarities but not her bad manners. Landon waited, not knowing where the conversation was going.

Denise greeted Bradley, then faced Landon again. "You seemed interested in my sister. I can tell by the way you looked at her."

Landon, who had been sipping on his glass of water, almost choked. "Excuse me?"

What was up with these Christmas sisters? Both women were gorgeous, but Denise was over the top with her assumption. *I appreciate good-looking women from afar from time to time.*

"I won't take up too much of your time because Gina and I can't be late to see *The Little Mermaid* at the Fox."

That explains why the sisters are dining here, Landon thought.

"She's single, thirty-two, and loves outings, which bore me. I'm sure you wouldn't refuse a date or two with an incredible woman if you were available. Just putting that bug in your ear. Now," she said, craning her neck and glancing toward her table, "I better get back before she suspects anything." Denise stood.

It took all the restraint Landon possessed not to laugh at this woman's ridiculous proposal. "I don't think your sister likes me," he joked but should have said, *I don't like her like that*. It would have been a lie.

"Oh, she does, but you'll have your work cut out for you." Denise gave him a knowing expression. "What you do with this information is up to you."

Was this woman really serious?

Was Landon seriously considering acting on the information he'd received? That was hilarious.

"Cool." Bradley grinned. "I wish the pretty girls at school would come up to me and ask me out like that."

"She didn't ask me out. Anyway, that was odd." Landon still didn't know what to make of that. Gina was beautiful, but because her older sister thought it was a good idea to ask her out, should he?

Ridiculous.

He was glad when their server placed their meals on the table. Landon said grace, then the two of them dug in.

"So, you going on a date?" Bradley grinned between bites.

Too dumbfounded to talk about it, Landon shrugged. "I have no idea."

Twenty minutes later, he spied the Christmas sisters walking out the door. The restaurant was packed and noisy, but he noticed them from across the room. They were beautiful but odd.

Refocusing on the purpose of this outing, Landon asked Bradley about his grades.

"They're alright." This time, it was the teenager who shrugged and looked away.

"If you want all the ladies, you have to make money, and with that comes book smarts. I can tutor you on certain subjects, but I want you to put in the time to learn."

"I'm going to be an athlete." Patting his chest proudly, he grinned. He wore a red-and-yellow striped shirt, the St. Louis City SC's colors, and a team cap, which Landon made him remove at the table.

"Being an athlete without book sense is like winning the lottery and losing it before you deposit it in your account."

Bradley twisted his lips. "You make it sound easy. It ain't. The teacher can't teach because the kids in my class are disruptive. They don't care about school."

"But you should. I understand the environment may not be the best for learning, but you have to press your way and pray every day that God walks into that classroom with you. Get with a tutor after school and see if there are YouTube videos on the subject so you can review lessons. Do you want to be an okay or outstanding soccer player?"

"I'm going to be a star." The teenager puffed out his chest, displaying a lopsided grin.

"You know the odds are against Black people because of our skin. You must prove yourself on and off the field and hire the best agent and publicity team… Have you heard of Ray Charles?"

Bradley frowned. "The blind guy?" He picked up a few fries that were left on his plate.

"Yes, the blind musician. I read he had people pay him in one-dollar bills so he wouldn't be cheated. A tedious task. I hope it worked. He didn't let his disability rob him of a good life."

There was a brief break in conversation as they enjoyed their meals.

Landon took a sip of his water. "You make it on a soccer team, and I'll be in the front-row seat."

"Bet. With the girlfriend?" He snickered.

"I don't have a girlfriend." Landon tugged on a few strands of his mustache, not wanting to return to the topic of romance. Once they finished their meals, he paid their tab and joined other fans heading toward City Park Stadium. Landon glanced at the Fox Theatre and the crowd in lines to see *The Little Mermaid*. Gina and her sister were somewhere in there.

He chuckled to himself about what Denise shared. If given a choice between the two events, although Landon wasn't a big soccer fan, soccer would win hands down. He had never been a theater, play, or symphony type of man.

Landon presented his phone at the stadium gate for the worker to scan their tickets, and Bradley's face lit up like a star. This made Landon smile, feeling good about making others happy.

Minutes after locating their seats, Bradley transformed himself into a play-by-play broadcaster. His knowledge and confidence blew Landon away.

At that moment, Landon realized he needed to do all he could to help Bradley reach his goal, even if it meant bribing him with a pricey season pass if the teenager invested in his academic studies. That had yet to be accomplished.

Out of nowhere, he asked, "So, are you going to take her out?" Bradley studied him with a mischievous smirk.

"Who?" Landon did not want to revisit this conversation.

"You know who. The pretty Christmas lady. The one who is going to be your girlfriend."

"I told you I don't have a girlfriend."

"Not yet." Bradley lifted his chin. "Christmas is coming early."

While Landon was in the office reviewing a project a week later, Granny Lonna called.

"Landon, I want you to go by that Christmas shop and see if items are in yet."

He groaned. "I doubt it. She said—"

"I don't care what they said," his grandmother snapped, which was unusual for the soft-spoken matriarch of his family. "Sometimes those one-of-a-kind pieces come in and out before anyone knows."

Granny Lonna was quiet. She was waiting him out. "Are you still here?"

"Yes, ma'am, I am."

"I expect you to do me this small favor. Want me to send you money?"

"Of course not. I don't…" Landon sighed heavily. It seemed like people were forcing him to be in Gina's presence. What did God have to say about this contact with Gina? They had differences of opinion. "Okay, I'll reach out now."

"Oh, goody. That's why you're my favorite grandson."

"Yes, I am." Her guilt trip was thick as they ended the call. Landon was busy with more pressing matters. He didn't have time for an extended lunch break because a recent sinkhole had caused a partial highway collapse in the city. Landon and his team had to survey the damage and make recommendations for the Missouri Department of Transportation and the sewer district workers to repair the highway section to reopen. Therefore, he decided to call instead. He looked up the number for Gina's company, and the call went to voicemail.

Great.

"Thanks for calling Christmas Tax Help for All Seasons. We're sorry we can't take your call because we're working with another customer. Please leave a message, and we'll reply within twenty-four hours. If you are a repeat client, feel free to email your W-2s and a list of your deductions, or you can drop off your taxes in our office. Thanks for calling. Have a blessed day."

Despite his frustration, Landon did admire her sultry but professional phone voice. Landon disconnected without leaving a message. After all, Gina had already told him not to expect anything soon. His grandmother wanted him to do what amounted to a stakeout, and she would check in with him two to three times to ensure Landon did it.

The best he could do was chance a visit to their office after he left work. If she was closed, at least he tried.

The inspection of the collapsed road showed extensive damage. The road was built on top of limestone and porous rocks, which wasn't safe and was a major disaster waiting to happen.

It took Landon longer than expected on the site. He was tired and wanted to go home when he returned to his office. For the sake of going to Christmas Tax Help for All Seasons, he would do a drive-by, knowing that Gina would be long gone home.

Traffic out of Clayton flowed, making his drive downtown smooth. Most of the businesses on Washington Avenue were dark, but not Gina's, even though it was almost seven-thirty. The lights inside and outside the office were lit like a Christmas tree, complete with garland. He hadn't noticed the decorations on his first visit.

Concerned, Landon parked and stepped out of his vehicle. Was it safe for her to be alone? Downtown St. Louis was deserted after six p.m. except for a few diners and restaurants catering to downtown city dwellers. Maybe she lived nearby or above the shop.

He walked up to the door and tried the knob. Locked. Landon exhaled. "Good." He peeked through the closed blinds, where he could see a glimpse of her working at a desk.

He tapped on the glass door. She looked up, then turned to view the security camera.

"May I help you?" she asked through the speaker.

"Hi, Miss Christmas. This is Landon Michaels."

She was quiet, then repeated, "How can I help, Mr. Michaels?"

Cautious. He admired that quality. "My grandmother was adamant about me checking back on angel ornaments."

"Unexpectedly, something did come in from the children's home, but can you come back another day? I was too busy to open the box. Sorry."

"Miss Christmas…" It wasn't his business, but he had to ask, "Are you safe by yourself? Do you want me to wait with you until you go home?"

"That's sweet, but with one call, I'll have an escort to my car."

Slipping his hands into his pants pockets, Landon knew his job was done, but he wasn't comfortable knowing she was vulnerable despite what she said.

"She's important to me," God whispered. *"Protect her as you would your sister. You both are my disciples."*

"Can you take my number? I'll wait in my car and escort you. I'll walk you."

"That's not necessary." Her voice was softer. "I'll be alright."

"Miss Christmas," he smiled, saying her name, "it's necessary for me. That's non-negotiable." He returned to his car and slid behind the wheel to wait.

Landon was hungry.

He was tired.

And he was on a stakeout to protect a woman he barely knew because it seemed like the right thing to do.

Chapter Three

Landon wasn't sure why he agreed to be a willing participant in Denise's scheme.

Gina Christmas didn't appear to be a woman who played coy. She was all about business and not interested. Her beauty attracted him, but her first impressions were lacking. She asked him for money—of sorts—something he never ever did. Whenever beggars asked for money, Landon would counter, asking them what they needed.

Drumming on the steering wheel, Landon chided himself for taking his grandmother's bait and showing up, so here he was, sitting in his car, demonstrating his chivalry to ensure she was safe. Almost an hour later, Landon saw her front door open. A short, bulky brother walked up when Landon was about to step out of his car. He stood anyway.

The man glared at him suspiciously, and Gina looked surprised to see him. Why? Didn't Landon tell her he would wait? He was a man of his word; otherwise, he would not have done it.

"Mr. Michaels," she said as she wrapped a dark sweater shawl with fringed fur balls around her shoulders.

"Please call me Landon." He nodded.

"Good night, Landon Michaels." Gina walked toward a parking lot on the side of the building, and the short guy kept stride with her.

That was cool…well, not really. Landon didn't like his good intentions to go unappreciated, so he slid back into his car and drove home.

The next day, Landon regrouped from his hurt feelings. He would continue this humiliation only at his grandmother's request. He couldn't stop thinking about Gina, and his grandmother hadn't stopped calling him for an update.

Then, somehow, Granny Lonna got his younger sister, Janay, involved in the conspiracy. She called him the following week while he was at work.

"Bro, we don't know how advanced her dementia is, so please try and find that ornament. Her Christmas could be in May, June, or July. We don't know," his sister said.

"This is ridiculous. I bought her two online. She asked where I got them from. When she learned it wasn't from that Christmas shop, which isn't a Christmas store, she told me to get my money back. It has to be from that place."

Janay sighed. "In that case. You have your assignment. Do I need to take a leave from my job to drive three hours from Kansas City to stay with you and bug the woman?"

"No, I got this." Landon gritted his teeth to contain his groan of frustration. He loved his only sibling, who was three years younger, and a carbon copy of Granny Lonna when she was the same age. Unfortunately, neither woman knew how to take no for an answer.

"I'm sure my smart engineering brother can construct a plan to be first on the contact list when a piece comes in." Janay sounded so confident that Landon could do it.

When a woman said no—and he wasn't referring to sex outside of marriage—Landon took it at face value, and Gina said no ornaments until July at the earliest. But she did say something had come in. Maybe a Black angel ornament was in the box.

This woman is single because she wants to be. Where did that thought come from?

His interest in Gina was about her safety. She was a sitting target for an assailant, he told himself and believed. "Lord, I know everything happens for a reason, even my grandmother's illness. I feel awkward bugging this woman. Please guide me, in Jesus' name. Amen." He prayed softly so others couldn't hear him in an office with an open space where conversations could easily be heard.

While retrieving a file on another sinkhole that would need an on-site inspection, Landon overheard his coworker lamenting he had done his taxes and had to pay.

A fleeting thought made Landon smile. He wondered if Gina would have been able to get him a refund. Landon learned to reduce his taxes by upping his 401(k) and church contributions. That helped, but more deductions were needed for a refund because he was single and earned a salary in a high-income bracket. He always had to pay, but not as much as Jeffrey Whitmore complained to the entire office.

Rubbing the hairs on his chin, Landon wondered if that was another angle he could use to stay at the top of the list and have the first peep at the Black angels when they arrived.

When Landon got home, he would gather his tax information for Miss Gina Christmas tomorrow.

The following evening was a bust. Landon proudly showed up to Christmas Tax Help for All Seasons with the required documents tucked in a manila envelope. She looked up from the desk and stared at him.

Her expression gave nothing away. No smile on her alluring lips. No sparkle in her brown eyes. She didn't look happy to see him. But Gina wasn't rude either. It is the perfect poker face to keep a player—or man—guessing.

Landon hid his humor because he was guessing what she was thinking.

She eyed him and then the envelope in his hands. "Hi, Landon. Can I help you?" Her tone was kind and patient, even though Landon assumed he was the last person she wanted to see.

"I need help with my taxes." He approached her desk. Landon did his best to portray an innocent look that kept him out of trouble as a boy.

"Do you?" She arched an eyebrow and twisted her lips to avoid smiling or showing annoyance with him. Landon didn't know which. "I'm sorry, I can't take on new clients. And I don't have any Christmas merchandise for your persistence." This time, she chuckled. "Sorry, but I'm busy. What about your previous tax preparer?"

Landon stalled, and she blinked twice, waiting for his answer. "I usually do them myself online." He bowed his head as if he was about to get in trouble.

Instead, she laughed. "I give you an A-minus for effort, but I have your card and will call you when something comes in."

"Oh. Why not an A-plus?"

"Because you're interrupting me from completing tax forms for my clients."

His roar of laughter caused a hint of a smile to pull at her lips.

"What about the box you haven't opened?" He remembered.

She tapped the pen on her desk. "There wasn't anything."

"Right. I'll leave." He backed away, admiring her beauty, then twirled around to head for the door.

"Landon, thank you for waiting outside for me that evening. I was touched." She patted her chest, showing off manicured nails about a half-inch long with a peachy spring color polish.

That did it for Landon. He felt appreciated for his chivalry. "You're welcome." He placed his hand on the doorknob and then looked over his shoulder. "Do you still have my business card?"

"Yes." She nodded. "It's in my drawer."

"Put my business and personal number in your phone. You don't have to wait for the merchandise to call me."

Gina exhaled after Landon left the building. It was hard to look the man in the eyes and not be affected by his handsomeness. She chuckled. His grandmother earned an A-plus for supporting the year-round Every Day is Christmas charity she'd founded. Gina knocked off half a point because his grandmother sent Landon, who tempted her senses and reminded her that she didn't have a special someone.

A week passed, and Gina saw his card in her drawer whenever she came into the office. He was a civil engineer. That meant he made good money, judging from the tax returns she had filed from clients in similar fields. And he was single? He was a good catch for some lady.

She wouldn't let herself be lured into the man's charm. Gina was a practicing Christian and had to wait on the Lord to send her a husband. She hoped it was soon. Her sister was getting tired of Gina dragging her to weekend events. Although their brother, John, was married, she and Denise hadn't been so fortunate to cross paths with a good guy like their brother.

Enough drifting. She had to refocus so it wouldn't be too late when she left. It was the end of March, and she had only a few weeks to keep the business running solo during tax season.

By Friday, Gina was grateful her sister had stopped by with lunch. Ordering food delivery was only a priority once she got a headache.

While the two munched on sub sandwiches on the corner of Gina's desk, she looked at the two plants that thrived from the sun's attention. "Why did I follow in our dad's and granddaddy's footsteps? I could have been a ballet dancer or chemist."

Denise laughed after taking a sip from her Styrofoam cup of lemonade, careful not to spill a drop on her white blouse. "Stick to what you know, kid. You are Daddy's little girl and wanted to do everything like our daddy." She chuckled.

"As the older sister, you should have rescued me." Gina squinted and took another bite. The chicken salad with grapes and pecans melted in her mouth. "This is so good."

"It's more fun to watch you tortured at tax time. You look exhausted. Are you sure you still want to go to *Shen Yun* this weekend?"

Before Gina could reply, the phone rang. Denise answered it so Gina could indulge in the first bite of the double chocolate chunk cookie that came with the meal.

Denise listened, then nodded. "Mr. Kincaid, let me check with Gina." She tapped the hold tab. "Is the Kin—"

"Done. Finished it last night. He can pick it up at any time. It should take five minutes, at the most, for him to review the numbers and then sign the form."

As Denise relayed the message, Gina was thankful for the impromptu receptionist who saved the call from defaulting to the company's voicemail, which she had to listen to at home.

Gina resumed reviewing the worksheet for the Fullers as she munched on the cookie. She had promised them their taxes would be done by today and ready for pickup tomorrow.

The door opened, and Gina sensed a familiar presence without looking up.

When Denise said too excitedly, "Oh, hi, Landon," it confirmed Gina's suspicions.

"Ladies." Landon's deep voice seemed to overpower the lobby.

"It's good to see you again. What brings you here?" Denise stood.

Was her sister flirting? Gina ignored their interaction and tried to stay focused. She was not about to have the IRS penalize her for miscalculating a client's estimated tax payment or refund. Her reputation and her family's company were on the line.

Landon was silent, although Gina could feel both her sister and his eyes on her.

"I came to—"

"To see if there are any new Christmas pieces," Gina said without looking up.

"Some came in yesterday," Denise said. "I haven't opened the box. We like to look at them before sending them to the charity for auction—a perk for being on the board. In the fall, we'll get some and put them on display for Christmas shoppers."

Gina let Denise and Landon check out the new pieces. Seeing what the talented children from the children's home created was one of Gina's favorite things to do, but not this tax season. She was short-staffed and had to put that on hold.

Her father worried about abandoning her. "I feel guilty for putting you in a bind," he had said when the doctor advised he couldn't postpone his back surgery any longer.

"Daddy, I don't want you to rush your healing and your physical therapy. I'll be fine," Gina remembered saying, thinking this would be easy.

Reality check. It hasn't been. She checked the time and prepared for the next client pickup, followed by a drop-off.

When the bell chimed, Gina stood and smiled at the Dixons. Although the young professional couple earned a lot of money, they were generous with their charitable contributions, which sometimes included Every Day is Christmas, to lower their tax liability. Gina never asked them for donations, and they never told her whenever they gave money. Only when the charity listed donor names did Gina recognize some were her clients.

"Come on back," Gina said, giving Denise and Landon a side-eye. After Gina was settled behind her dad's desk, she faced the couple and opened their tax file to verify their deductions before revealing the amount they would have to pay the IRS.

"Well, that's less than last year," Jade said to her husband, Rick, who agreed.

After they signed their forms, Gina thanked them for their business.

Rick pulled out his phone to send the payment for her services to the company electronically.

As she walked the Dixons out, her next client walked in to drop off his taxes. She was surprised Landon was still there and Denise, too, admiring canvas art. It wasn't an ornament but an angel on a gold metallic background and white organza for the wings. *Stunning.*

Denise looked over her shoulder at Gina and smiled.

Even Landon smiled, and Gina's heart fluttered.

Would that piece suffice for his grandmother instead of an ornament? If so, his mission was complete. Landon

Michaels had found what he wanted. She would direct him toward the charity for the transaction.

That's it. There is nothing here to make him come back. Why did that realization make her sad?

Chapter Four

Landon liked getting to know Denise while Gina was busy, but he was more interested in Gina sharing what she wanted him to know about her than her sister giving away all of Gina's secrets.

Denise was a sales rep to the core. If Gina had a price tag, Landon was ready to buy. According to Denise, Gina was the package deal that only a foolish man would let get away.

Amused, Landon stopped her with a timeout gesture. "I can see why you're in sales. I'm about ready to purchase, but I'm curious why both of you are still on the market."

"One blessing at a time." Denise's expression reminded him of Gina. "We are a Bible-believing family. If I bless others first, my blessing is coming. That was the basis for our charity." She whispered, "Trust me. I am a great catch, but I have to want to be caught."

Gina seemed suspicious about their mumbling, so Denise cleared her throat and handed him the delicate artwork.

He examined the canvas's background in brush strokes of white and off-white. The angel was constructed of glitter, organza, and other material he couldn't identify. It was one-of-a-kind from an artist with skill and vision. It didn't resemble a child's craft. "It doesn't have a price tag on it. How much?"

"Make an offer," Denise said with a raised eyebrow.

Was this supposed to be a game? "*Hmmm*. I'll give you twenty dollars."

Denise nodded. "Good starting bid."

"Bid? Okay, it's for the children. Twenty-five." He shrugged and went in Gina's direction. He'd preferred to make this transaction with her.

"I got twenty-five. Do I hear thirty?" Denise was hustling him.

"This isn't an auction," Landon told her. "I can't bid against myself."

The woman was in her element, and she seemed confident and efficient. "You might want to rethink that. This is an auction because other contributors are willing to buy sight unseen. Since you don't know how this works, I'll let you have it at a bargain." She grinned in triumph as he slipped two twenties out of his wallet.

She made no gesture to give him change. "We're not finished."

"Huh? I need to get back to work." He checked the time. He had a planning meeting in an hour and a half.

"Me too. One hundred, and you have a bargain." Denise smiled.

"What?" He tried to lower his voice so as not to disturb Gina. Landon thought forty dollars was generous. He had no idea of the value of art.

At the end of the haggling, Landon paid seventy-five dollars. Surely, that was a tax write-off.

"Sold, and for your generosity, I have two tickets," she whispered, "to *Shen Yun*. And for the record, I can't conduct auctions because it's a conflict of interest since it's our charity, but that was fun, and I'll make sure the foundation manager gets the proceeds."

"What?" Landon shook his head in disbelief. This sister was cunning. "She who?"

"*Shhh*. It's a performance of Chinese culture, costumes, music, and dance."

No was on his tongue when Denise said, "I got these tickets from a client, and my sister loves these performances. Of course, you have to spring for dinner because it will be a date."

This woman was over-the-top scary. Landon was too dumbfounded to speak. First, she had weaseled him to overpay for this Black angel—he didn't let go of his money that easily.

Now, she had set him up on a date without his permission. But he wasn't complaining. Landon wanted to find out if all the things Denise said about her sister were true, like eating cereal at night because she didn't have time in the mornings or having three favorite colors and wearing them all the time in some variety.

"It's this weekend, so you might want to cancel if you have other plans. The tickets can only be used to take my sister, so if you have a girlfriend, I rescind my offer."

Shaking his head, Landon chuckled in disbelief. Who was running his life—him or this woman? "Not interested." Did he say that?

"Liar. I'm trying to help you out here. I saw the way you looked at my sister. She is more than a pretty face."

Among other things, he remembered his unexpected attraction to Gina the first time he saw her. After the pleasantries, they clashed on charity work. But she seemed to have won via Denise since Landon handed over his money without knowing how it would support the child.

"These tickets are valued at two hundred and fifty dollars. Don't let them go to waste." With that said, she laid them on the counter, inched them closer to him, walked away, and kissed her sister goodbye. "Don't work too hard, sis. Bye, Landon Michaels."

Taking a seat, Landon tried to figure out how he had just been ambushed.

Gina looked up at him when she ended the call with a client and asked, "Can I help you? My sister sold you the Christmas piece that came in, which she shouldn't have because that's the charity manager's job to assign an opening bid price, which probably would have been more. But the money will get to them. Trust me. Thank you for supporting Every Day Is Christmas."

His mind captured her smile for instant playback. This was a refreshing moment. Although Denise was entertaining, Gina fascinated him. He slipped the tickets in his pants pocket. He needed to leave but had this small window to speak with Gina. "You're welcome. I do think it's overpriced—"

She cut him off. "Can you put a price on investing in children's future?" She didn't allow him to answer. "No. Most of our ornaments and Christmas-themed items are crafts by talented children trying to earn money for softball uniforms, piano lessons, or whatever creative ventures spark their curiosity."

Landon held up his hands in surrender. "I apologize. As you saw a few weekends ago, my philosophy on investing in children differs from yours. I like to spend time with them as a mentor."

"That's time I don't have," she told him. "I like my weekends to be my own."

"I hope you will after April fifteenth. What do you do for fun?"

"My sister and I hang out mostly, or occasionally, I'll meet up with a couple of friends."

Yes, the reason for Denise's ambush. Landon exhaled, not sure if that was his open door. "I have two tickets to see a Chinese performance, *Chen Won*. Would you like to go?"

"*Shen Yun*?" She didn't hide her surprise or delight. "I'm sorry, but I already have a date."

"Right. If it's with your sister, she gave me your tickets."

"What?" She stood. Gina was not happy. Her nostrils flared, and she stomped her feet hard enough to break a heel, but it didn't give.

Landon stepped closer to the desk. "We've been ambushed. If you don't mind, let's get to know each other over this date."

"Is this a date?" She jutted her chin and folded her arms.

"Bad choice of words. So it's not a formal date because a man never allows a woman to pay. Never."

Gina was quiet, and her features softened. "Okay. I'll meet you there."

"I'd rather pick you up."

"It's not a date." She smiled as her next client walked in.

"You win for now." Landon walked out the door to return to his job.

Chapter Five

Gina phoned her parents on Saturday morning. Despite the anticipation of another amazing Chinese performance, she was nervous Landon would be there as her date or escort, a man she didn't want to be attracted to. "Track my whereabouts."

She told them how Denise had given the tickets to a man she knew little about to be Gina's date. "I'll pay her back! She knows how much I look forward to going, and she set me up."

Her mother, Patrice Christmas, always played the mediator between Gina and her sister. "Denise is a good judge of character. She wouldn't put you in harm's way. And we know God can dispatch an army of angels to protect you." She was on speakerphone.

Gina's dad, Ray, was in the background. "And you did say yes."

"It was a conspiracy." Gina tried not to fume as she got ready.

"Find out as much as you can about him. A photo ID is even better," Ray said.

"He did give me his business card. His name is Landon Michaels—"

"*Highway to Heaven*," her mom said as if she was playing a game show.

"Right. His grandmother was a fan." Gina chuckled. "He's a civil engineer with Claymount Engineering Company."

"That's a good job," her father said. "You need to find out if he's paying alimony or child support."

"Your father has a point. I pray that my girls would step into the pathway of a good-looking, God-fearing, family-oriented man. Pray for discernment. There are a lot of copycat Christians out there."

"Don't I know it," she mumbled before they ended the call.

Gina loved her older sister, but she was ready to strangle her when she found out what Denise had done, and all Gina needed was one minute in between appointments to threaten her. "And I thought you were auctioning off artwork. Instead, you were auctioning me off!" She didn't hide her hurt feelings.

"Girl, please. Landon is doing us a favor. He wouldn't have accepted the tickets and asked you out if he wasn't attracted to you. You could have said no if you didn't want to go with him."

There was no way Gina wanted to miss the performance. Hopefully, he would sleep through it so she could enjoy it without interruption. Between nervousness and attitude, Gina wasn't in a forgiving mood to let Denise off the hook. She called her while getting dressed.

Denise answered in a cheerful tone. "Are you excited?"

So her sister was playing games. "Yes, to see the performance. No to Landon being there with my ticket. I don't know this man."

"You will after today," Denise said in a sing-song tone. "He has my stamp of approval."

"Girl, it's one day shy of April first, and we're too old for April Fool's jokes. I can't believe you did this."

"Stop protesting and get pretty. I'm dropping you off, so you don't have to drive. If you're uncomfortable with Landon taking you home afterward, call me, and I'll come and get you."

"This is a matinee, and I can park in a garage."

"Not by yourself."

"Says the woman now concerned about my safety."

After they ended the call, Gina showered, applied her makeup, and eyed her clothes in her closet. Why was she second-guessing her attire? With spring on the horizon, she had planned to wear her powder blue dress and duster set, but now?

She tapped her chin, careful not to smudge her makeup. "Why am I obsessing over what to wear? Landon is taking me by default—or ambush, as he called it."

Gina liked attending cultural events. They made her appreciate her diversity. She piled her hair on top of her head, looped earrings through her ears, and threw a kiss at her reflection as her doorbell rang.

She peeped out the window to double-check that Denise had not handed over Gina's address as part of her match-making mission.

Denise's navy blue Benz was in the driveway. Of all the professionals her sister worked with as a sales rep,

Gina was surprised she didn't have someone special in her life. But payback was coming one day soon enough.

In truth, dating didn't seem to be on a woman's side, regardless of her looks, education, and confidence. Gina slipped on her duster and opened the door.

Her sister stood there, squinting and scrutinizing her, then bobbed her head. "I approve. You look pretty. I hope you enjoy your date." Denise grinned as the two walked to her car.

"According to Mr. Michaels," Gina paused to slide into the car and snap her seatbelt, "this is not a date because he's not paying."

"Ooh, a man with integrity. I like him even more." Grinning, Denise steered her car to the highway to Stifel Theatre.

Once Denise was downtown, she maneuvered her car through the crowd to get Gina as close as possible to the entrance.

"I'll jump out here. It's not a far walk. I hope Landon doesn't stand me up with those tickets."

"Me either. Enjoy."

Gina stepped out and joined the others at the light to cross the street. As she climbed the stairs with everyone else, she looked up, made eye contact with Landon, and almost tripped.

Landon stood magnificent in a tailored royal blue suit that had heads turning. His tie and pocket handkerchief were a contrast but color coordinated. Suddenly, Gina felt attendees had parted a path for them.

He descended quickly toward her to catch her before she fell. His strong hand lifted her with ease, and Landon guided her up the remaining stairs to the landing. "You look beautiful," he said as his eyes twinkled in appreciation.

Sucking in her breath, Gina thanked him. She felt beautiful, hoping the concealer camouflaged the dark circles and tired lines around her eyes. When was the last time she was given a compliment? Not during tax season, for sure.

The two entered the theater after passing through a metal detector. Landon showed their tickets to the usher, who guided them up the stairs.

"I have to say I feel uncomfortable accepting the tickets when I could have paid for them myself."

His admission made Gina respect him more. "Thank you for saying that."

With his hand on her arm, Landon kept her steady as they climbed the stairs to another level.

"Did you want any popcorn or something to drink? If you let me, I plan to take you to dinner afterward."

Gina didn't commit. She hoped Denise didn't plan that, too.

As expected, Denise had gotten them perfect seats. Landon asked again if she wanted anything. She declined, zooming in on couples, some with matching colors, who seemed happy for the outing. *Do Landon and I look like a couple?* she wondered.

The lights faded to dark as the commentators appeared on stage. The woman spoke in Chinese, and the male translated in English.

"You're going to love this," Gina whispered as she braced to be wowed. The large screen unfolded and stretched across one end of the stage to another. Soon, the battle on the virtual screen seemed to jump onto the stage, and the story began.

Surprisingly, Landon seemed just as engaged whenever she glanced at him. Gina was impressed.

When the intermission was announced an hour and a half later, Landon was speechless.

"Impressed, huh?"

"Yes." He looked surprised and smiled at her.

Gina blushed. He seemed nice enough to get to know.

Two and a half hours later, by the end of the show, Landon couldn't stop singing the show's praises. It was as if he met Jesus.

Without asking for permission, Landon held her hand as if it were natural between them while he guided her out of the auditorium. She didn't protest his touch, which made her hand tingle. Landon seemed aware of the spark and squeezed her hand before she could remove it.

They walked through the doors outside, and Landon faced her. "This is where it could end or begin with us."

Us. She wanted to say there wasn't an "us" but held her peace.

"We can go to dinner, and I'll take you home, or I'll wait with you for your sister to pick you up, which is a bad choice. Or you can allow me a date without interference from your sister."

Gina tilted her head as she studied him for the first time. She noticed the slight dimple when he was about to smile but didn't. His stare was intense yet warm, never wavering as people moved around them. "Since you gave me three choices, I'll pick numbers one and three."

She giggled.

He frowned.

"I didn't know I gave you so many choices." He reached for her hand and squeezed. "So what did you agree to?"

"I'm an accountant. Numbers are my game. One is for you to take me to dinner and then home, which will be my parents' house. Heads up, they have tracking on my phone and probably have a drone flying overhead."

He glanced up and squinted in the sky. "Tell me you're kidding."

"I am, but put nothing past my family. And yes to going on a real date. Any man who enjoys aerobatics during a fight scene can't be all bad."

His hearty laugh rumbled from his stomach. "Why don't you wait here, and I'll get the car and bring it around?"

Gina nodded, then tracked his swagger down the stairs before he blended in with the crowd.

She sighed. If today's "not a date" outing turned into the "best date ever," Gina would owe Denise big time. If not, Denise wouldn't hear the last of it.

Chapter Six

Landon had been on two blind dates in his life, both disastrous. Today was a setup date, and it had a different feel. Not only was he engrossed in the performance, the company was stunning.

Gina was carefree, relaxed, and beaming with happiness as she followed the show—the opposite of the all-business woman he first met.

"Do you have a preference or food allergies?" he asked after he helped her into his car.

"That's considerate of you to ask, but I don't," she said as her phone chimed with an alert. She looked down and laughed, then tapped away her response. Gina turned to him. "That was our matchmaker."

"Tell her I owe her more for those tickets." Landon chuckled. "I had a good time." And that surprised him.

"She didn't pay for them. Denise gets them free from her clients all the time."

So, the joke was on him. When her sister told him the value of the tickets, Landon felt obligated not to let them go to waste.

Once they arrived at the Thai restaurant, Gina seemed delighted in his choice.

At the entrance, an unkempt man dressed in torn clothes, worn brown boots, and an oversized dirty khaki coat looked at them. His eyes pleaded with them not to ignore him.

"Can you spare some change?" He stretched out his dirty palm.

Landon moved his mouth from side to side. This man needed food, not a handout. "What can I get you here to eat?"

His eyes lit up. "Sir, I can eat anything. I'm so hungry."

The raw pain in the beggar's voice made Landon ache. "Done." He touched Gina's back to guide her up the stairs, but she didn't budge as she fumbled with her wallet.

"That's not necessary. I got him," Landon tried to dissuade her.

She jutted her chin. "He asked for change." Gina handed him a ten-dollar bill.

Landon said nothing as the man accepted it. *Watch him disappear now*, he thought.

The man didn't need Landon to order him food. Gina gave him money. A tear fell from the man's eye with his whispered thanks.

Judgment belongs to Me! God thundered.

Landon repented silently.

"Come on. He's waiting on his order," Gina said and stepped toward the doors. Once they were shown to their table, Landon kept his word. "Although we're eating here, I would like to place a to-go order of whatever you can cook fast," he told their hostess. "Please add bottled water and dessert." Then he nodded for Gina. She ordered a chicken cashew wheat noodle dish while Landon's mouth watered for teriyaki chicken and rice.

When the woman left to do his bidding, Gina smiled. "That was nice of you."

Landon accepted the compliment, but his mind was still on God's rebuke even though Landon's generosity was worth more than ten bucks. "Tell me, what attracted you to accounting?"

"It's on the building—Christmas Tax Help for All Seasons. My grandfather had smart sense. Without a formal education, he was self-taught in managing money. He could easily have been a financial advisor in his day. Instead, he showed people how to save money on their taxes and save money, period. My dad went to school, and he helped grow the business. I wanted to be like them."

Landon admired that Gina was down to earth. "Is that why you started the charity?"

"Oh no." Gina shook her head and waved her finger while leaning forward. Were her eyes always that alluring, or was this the first time he noticed? Landon wanted to meet her midway as if she was about to whisper a secret, but Gina smirked instead. "It's my turn for the next question. What do you have against charities?"

Mood killer. He cleared his throat and guarded his words but couldn't sugarcoat his conviction. "Accountability. Look at where the U.S. and other countries have poured money, like Haiti. On the surface, the money reached the people, but in the long term, their needs were never met. I would rather be hands on the ground there, making a difference, rebuilding their lives. I mentor—"

"The teenager I met?" Her lips curved into a smile.

"Yes. He's my neighbor." He nodded. "Bradley needs encouragement from a mentor, not money thrown at him that he doesn't know how to save." Landon stopped. He had said enough. She disagreed with his assessment, but he felt strongly about that.

Their server returned with the to-go bag, and Landon double-checked that cutlery was included. "Thank you." He excused himself, took the bag, and headed outside to the front, half expecting the homeless man to be gone, but he was there. He waited obediently by the door as if he was a lost pet.

He's My lost sheep. Feed My sheep. Not only substance but spiritual manna, God whispered.

The man's eyes watered as Landon approached. He squatted and handed over the bag. "What's your name?"

"William." He bowed his hands and gave thanks with the sign of the cross.

Landon stood, reached into his back pocket for his wallet, and pulled out a business card. "Call me if you need a job, food, or shelter. I know of resources that can help. Most of all, read your Bible. Do you have one?"

William nodded but didn't stop eating, so Landon backed up to give the man space. "Read it, and God will send the help."

Landon prayed for him, then pivoted and returned to the restaurant with a confident smile. His donation was more practical.

Giving is not a competition, God whispered.

Gina looked hopeful when he returned empty-handed. "Was he still there?"

"Yes, ma'am. William was waiting for his meal." He sat down, again chastened by the Lord. Landon would have to work on his attitude. He regrouped and focused on his date. "You were about to tell me about your charity."

"Yes." Gina beamed. "Every Day is Christmas is a 501(c)(3) tax-exempt entity. The money supports children every day, not just around the holidays. Would you like to see our books?" Gina had switched to business mode.

This time, it wasn't a turn-off but an attractive feature. "I would never question a CPA."

"Good." She grew concerned. "Do you really need help filing your taxes?"

"Nah. It was just an excuse to see you." That made her smile. "I normally file online. I always owe, so I usually wait until a few days before the deadline." Landon shrugged.

"I'm sure our company can find you more deductions." She paused when their food arrived. "Thank you," she and Landon said to their server simultaneously, then looked at each other.

Landon held open his hands and waited for her to rest hers in his, then bowed his head to say grace. "Lord, we give thanks for today and the food prepared for us. Sanctify it, remove the impurities, and help us remember to serve others who are hungry, in Jesus' name. Amen."

"Amen," she repeated.

He was surprised she offered him a taste as they sampled their dishes. He grinned. "I will get that next time."

"Will I be your dining companion?"

If she was baiting him, Landon took it. "Definitely."

So, she did possess some of the same sass as Denise. He liked it.

They ate in silence until Gina dabbed her lips. "You're a soccer fan."

"Not really, but my neighbor is fanatical about it, so I bribed Bradley with tickets to keep his grades up."

Gina tilted her head and studied him. "Do you always do things you don't want to do?"

"Never." He gave her a serious expression. "Everything I do has a purpose—with good intentions."

"What's the story about the ornament that brought you to my office in the first place?"

"She loved it, but it wasn't what she wanted. My grandmother has dementia. She's obsessed with Christmas ornaments, especially Black angels from your charity, and she's relentless in getting her way. We don't know where her mind will be at Christmas, so I want to give it to her while she can enjoy it."

"Oh, that's sweet." Gina reached across the table, grasped his hand, and squeezed. "I'll be praying for her."

The sincerity in her voice made him choke. His Granny Lonna would like her, and he smiled. "Thanks. I do have one request," he said as she picked up her fork and began to eat again. "You have a few more weeks before the tax season deadline, and you're working until it's dark outside. Do you have a problem with me coming to your office every evening and waiting so I can walk you to your car?"

Gina's jaw dropped. "Every evening?"

"Every," he confirmed.

His request had rendered her speechless. *Good.* He would wait for her answer.

And it finally came when her brown eyes lit with happiness. "Okay."

"There's one more thing." Landon came with demands.

Now, she waited for him to continue.

"Do you mind giving me your number?"

Laughing, she patted her chest. "You got me with your serious expression. Whew. Hand me your phone, and I'll put it in."

Landon removed it from his belt clip and placed it in her palm. She tapped in her number, and he heard a ringtone coming from inside her phone and inside her purse. He liked Gina Christmas. Now they both had each other's number.

He also thanked Granny Lonna and Denise for the setup.

Unfortunately, it was time to go as they saw new patrons come, eat, and leave. He could no longer stall their outing.

"Are you ready for me to take you home?" Landon held his breath. Did he pass the inspection?

She smiled. "Yes, until next time. You can drop me off at their home."

Since when were the Christmases outdoor people? Yet, they were all outside at once. Her mother fussed with her already meticulous flower bed near the porch. Her father sat in the rocker as if it were the norm when it was usually her mom's perch. The kicker was Denise, who had decided to clean out her car's interior—all suspicious activities for her family.

Rolling her eyes, she shook her head.

"I guess this is our destination." Landon chuckled.

This looked like a coordinated surveillance. They must have been tracking her phone for real. "What gave it away?"

"Denise. She's waving hard as if she's flagging down a race car driver at a checkpoint."

Landon parked his SUV, and in seconds, he stepped out and opened her door. His attention made her blush.

"It looks like you two had a good time." Denise was the first to speak as they approached her family.

"I did," Gina and Landon said in unison and looked at each other.

Landon stepped on the first stair and extended his hand to her father. "Mr. Christmas, it's nice to meet you. Your daughter is doing a great job running the business in your absence."

Ray beamed. "Glad to hear it. I hate I left her in a bind."

Gina's heart skipped at Landon's boast. "That's nice of Landon to say, but I'll be glad when midnight on April fifteen comes."

Her mother squinted and scrutinized Landon as if he were fresh produce, then invited him inside. "I'm Patrice, Gina's mother. Let's chat for a few minutes."

Gina groaned and whispered, "Are you ready for this?"

"Your sister has made me ready for anything." They laughed and followed her family inside to the living room.

While Mom and Dad commandeered Landon, Denise pulled her into the kitchen.

"Well?" Denise squinted and grinned. "Details."

"Surprisingly, I had a nice time. Magnificent performance and a wonderful…escort."

"It was a date, girl." Denise began shaking her hips and moving her arms to a muted beat. It was a goofy rendition of an African dance. "It looks like Dad's impressed."

"I am, too."

A couple of hours later, Gina had learned more about Landon, his career, and his family than she had on her date. Her parents were polite but ruthless.

She tried to rescue him. "Mom and Dad, Landon has to go. Tomorrow is Sunday and church." Gina was ready to go home and unwind. She reminded her father that he needed his rest, and so did she since two more weeks were left in the tax season.

"You're right, sweetheart." Ray stood with Landon and her mother's assistance.

"I like you, Landon. Let's keep it that way. You said you would check on my daughter, and I'm holding you to it."

Her father's stern expressions were frightening as a child and now.

Landon seemed unfazed by the unspoken threat. "I will."

The two shook hands.

Gina said goodbye minutes later, ushering Denise out the door to take her home. Otherwise, she would be interrogated, lectured, or married off. Not today.

Chapter Seven

Sunday morning, Landon stared at his phone, willing it to ring from Gina with an invite to her church worship service.

Nothing.

He couldn't wait any longer, so he showered, ate, and dressed casually to attend his church, Kingdom Come.

Since yesterday, he hadn't been able to get Gina out of his head—her eyes, lips, and perfume. God created her with every beautiful ingredient available. Regarding personal matters, Landon liked to remain tight-lipped around his family. He preferred not to hear others' opinions on what he should and shouldn't do in relationships.

There was one person whose opinion Landon would consider. His best friend, Terrell Sims, was an exception. They had developed a bond as close as siblings while attending Howard University. Although the two had chosen different career paths—engineering and law—they shared the same taste in ethnic foods, social activities, and a similar mindset.

Landon needed to run the scenario about Gina by Terrell, whom he planned to call later after visiting Granny Lonna after church.

With his Bible in one hand and car keys in the other, the doorbell delayed him from leaving for church. He opened his door to see Bradley on his porch, balancing a soccer ball on one foot. "What's up?"

"Nothing. Did you go on a date with the Christmas lady?" Bradley snickered.

"Huh?" Landon frowned. "What makes you think I went on a date?"

"I saw you leave yesterday wearing a suit. It wasn't Sunday, and you didn't come back until almost dark. You were gone almost six hours."

Landon's jaw dropped. "What are you, a neighborhood watch captain now or something? And your math is off."

Bradley shrugged. "Nope, just observant. So is she your girlfriend? If you take…"

"Goodbye, Bradley." Landon sighed. "Unless you're going to church with me, which you should be going with your grandmother anyway, we'll chat later." Landon grinned, closed the front door, and walked through his kitchen to the garage door.

There was no way Landon was going to take advice from a teenager.

———— ❦ ————

True to his word and commitment to Gina's father, Landon arrived at Christmas Tax Help for All Seasons every evening, bearing food—either delicious leftovers he had cooked and made extra for her or scrumptious carryout.

"You've got skills," Gina teased him on the third day.

"I told you I like to eat." He blessed their food and set up shop near the nook so he wouldn't distract her as she worked.

Although Landon was quiet, his presence distracted her. He was a caring, considerate, and humble man.

On Friday, Landon came without food.

"Hey, I'm hungry." Disappointed, Gina pouted.

"I'm sure you are." He grinned. "I thought I would take you out for a late dinner."

"So," she said, tilting her head and squinting at him, "you're telling me to hurry up?"

"Nope." Landon slipped his hands in his pants pockets and pulled out some treats he had grabbed from the vending machine at work. "Take your time, then hurry up. I'm starving, too."

"Oh, goodie." They laughed before Gina turned away and focused on the Schedule A worksheet.

After an hour, Gina shut down her computer and quietly grabbed her things to go.

Stretched in a chair with his ankles crossed and eyes closed, Landon said, "Finished so soon?"

Gina couldn't help but smile at his concern. She usually didn't leave until after seven on most evenings, and it was only five-thirty. "I'm hungry, too. I'll work on it this weekend from home." She yawned as Landon stood to assist her with her duster.

On the first evening, Landon had informed her mail carrier neighbor, Fred, that his escort services were no longer needed. Territorial, Gina mused, but it was flattering.

Fred wasn't fazed and refused to leave without Gina's permission. As if to irk Landon, Fred flexed his muscles. "Okay, Miss Christmas, but I'll be watching him to make sure he's not a Grinch or Scrooge trying to steal Christmas."

Gina had wanted to laugh, but Landon didn't appear to think it was funny, so she faked a serious expression and planned to tell Denise later. They both would crack up.

After she set the security alarm and turned the key, she and Landon walked to the side parking lot.

"What do you have a taste for?" Landon asked as he opened her door.

"Surprise me with something light," she said as they strolled to her car. She was tired but didn't want to pass up the opportunity to spend some downtime with Landon.

"Okay. Follow me, and drive carefully." He closed the door and then walked to his vehicle.

While she waited, Gina started her engine and prayed, *Lord, protect my heart. Don't let me invest it, if he's not who You have for me, in Jesus' name. Amen.* Minutes later, she pulled out of the parking lot, trailing Landon.

Feeling better since she had prayed when they arrived at The Food Joint, Gina relaxed in her seat and enjoyed the easy conversation that didn't center around taxes. Couples, friends, and family gathered at various-sized square tables in the spacious restaurant. Landon's features were mesmerizing, and it was hard not to stare. "I've always wanted to try this place, but Denise was never interested in dishes from other countries."

"I've never eaten food my taste buds haven't enjoyed." He smacked his lips.

"I have another question to ask." When Landon nodded, Gina continued, "Do you attend church, or are you a practicing Christian?" That should have been the first question.

He didn't answer right away. "I used to think there wasn't a difference, but I surrendered by repenting and being baptized in Jesus' name. My eyes were opened to see everyone doesn't love God in the same way."

"How so?" This was an interesting discussion.

"Before I became serious about my salvation, I was the type of person who straddled the fence with God to do just enough to make it to heaven. Now, I don't want to play with God."

"True. There's a lot of playing church going around."

Landon quieted and shook his head. "I can't believe a woman as smart, beautiful, kind, and a lover of God is single. You're the whole package—my package."

Had Gina heard right? He said, *my*. "Ooh, I've dated men from the church, professionals, and even tried some blind dates. This is my first setup."

"Mine too." He touched her hand. "We are in this together."

They paused when their server returned to refill their water glasses.

"It always seemed I had to settle." Gina shrugged. "Let me say, I never had the complete package."

"What about now?" Landon seemed to challenge her.

"Too early to tell."

"Ouch. But fair enough." He grinned. Gina's truthfulness was as attractive as her smile.

"I'm being honest. I don't know how different you are from others in the past. Looks… Wow, you've got the copyright on that."

"Good to know." Landon snickered.

Gina counted on her fingers. "Education and job. Any woman should make that a prerequisite."

"As well as a man."

"Excuse me?" *See, this is why I said it's too early to tell. This man is about to miss a checkmark on my list.*

"Unless a woman has a family to nurture, why wouldn't she want to work? If you have any insight, please let me know. My parents reared my sister and me to be responsible for ourselves; getting that first job as a teenager at a grocery store taught us about being responsible and dependable no matter the position. It's the same way I want to rear my children…when I have them."

Okay, I was too fast to judge him. Gina relaxed against her chair and listened. "And what about your wife when you have one?"

"We'll have a conversation and come to an agreement. I make good money, but daycare is expensive. It might not make sense for both of us to work. However, I have parents. I wish my Granny could help." He became quiet and reflective.

What was he thinking? Gina didn't want him to stop now.

"So if *your wife* wants to work, you won't demand that she stay home?" Gina squinted. This was better than playing checkers or chess, which she didn't know how to play.

"Again, my wife and I will work out the details. Seeing my sister struggle to prove herself as a successful Black woman in the workplace to break barriers hasn't been easy for me to not come to her defense."

Gina smiled. Her big brother, John, acted as her and Denise's protector growing up, but he'd married young and moved away.

"Janay's worked hard to earn respect. I wouldn't want to see anyone, including her husband, take away something she's earned. It has to be her decision to walk away." The conviction behind his words made Gina move him up a notch on her checklist board.

Landon Michaels was husband material.

Chapter Eight

It took a week before Landon's friend, Terrell, called him back. "I need counsel, bro. The text messages didn't help," Landon said while he muted the baseball game and activated his recliner backward to stretch out. They needed to catch up.

"Based on your messages, I have no advice regarding relationships." Terrell chuckled. "Seriously, though, it sounds like Gina is someone special. There's another attorney I met at a conference with the last name of Christmas. Wonder if they're related..."

"Terrell, I don't care about who she's related to. I need help processing what I'm feeling."

"Alright. Tell me how you met her. Give me the long version."

Landon started from the beginning, with Granny Lonna's quest for a Black angel ornament, and ended with volunteering to be Gina's bodyguard. "Whatever I don't finish at my office, I bring and work on it while waiting for her. I call it our quiet time together." Landon grinned. He had no complaints about the arrangement.

"Wow. *Hmmm*." Terrell was silent. "Are you afraid?"

"Of what?" Landon laughed to hide his nervousness. He was not confident about how Gina controlled his thoughts with little effort. Was it her honesty or the way she looked at him? Landon didn't know.

"Do you think she's playing games or something to lure you in? My counsel is to talk to God about this unfamiliar territory."

"Yeah. You're right. She's genuine and speaks her mind. Her sass is attractive."

For the next hour, they discussed flattering and undesirable traits from their past girlfriends and compared them to Gina. His friend's advice caused Landon to do the mental workout. "Unless you don't think you can bounce back from a breakup, Gina Christmas is worth your investment."

"First, we have to be in a relationship. Okay, Attorney Sims, I think I've taken up enough of your time. Don't bill me."

Terrell roared with laughter. "Be cautious, man. Please keep your eyes open for blemishes in her character that aren't easily concealed like women who use makeup. Character. Pray on this. Because I deal with facts clearly, this is a matter of heart and mind. Talk to you later."

Have you asked Me to lead you? God whispered. *I know the plans I have for you…*

No, I haven't. Landon knew the scripture in Jeremiah 29:11.

In his thirty-five years, Landon never felt emotionally out of control until his eyes locked on Gina, and his heart surrendered, then recalculated. During those quiet times at her office, Landon liked to imagine what a relationship would look like.

Landon was over the casual dating and the occasional dinners in his life. He needed a purpose that only a wife and a family could bring. *Lord, if Gina isn't part of Your plan for me, show me sooner rather than later.*

God was silent.

This was when Landon could have used a cryptic message like "watch and pray," but nothing.

Gina felt like she had barely survived tax season when April 15 arrived.

Landon walked through the door with an engaging, lopsided grin. His eyes sparkled, and a slight dimple flashed at her. It was the happiest she had ever seen him. "Congratulations. You did it. Let's celebrate!" He presented a small white cake box in his hands.

She eyed him before accepting the gift, then slowly opened it as if something would fly out like those surprise explosion boxes she'd seen on social media. Inside was a white-iced cake decorated with an image to resemble a U.S. Treasury refund check made payable to Gina Christmas. *Priceless* was written in the amount box. *Congratulations on a successful tax season* in the memo.

Touched by his thoughtful gesture, Gina was choked with emotion. Her vision blurred. Landon had seen firsthand all the hard work she had done to make it a successful year without her dad.

"*Awww.* Thank you." She placed the cake on her desk and stood on her toes to kiss his cheek softly.

His response was more intense than she anticipated. He wrapped his strong arms around her, pulled her closer, and delivered a sweet kiss.

Pulling away, Gina panted for air. "Whoa. Sorry. That was my fault. I shouldn't have started that."

"Not for me. I've been waiting for that kiss, and if you *could* take it back, I'd fight you for it." Folding his arms, he frowned at her. "Tell me why you feel it was a mistake."

Gina fumbled with her fingers and looked away, stalling to answer. Her first distraction was the Christmas nook, which was bare—she would have to stock up on goodies—and then her messy desk, where the cake box lay. She sighed.

Her attraction had tempted him to respond with that passion. *Cool it, girl!* "Landon, although we're alone, God is our chaperone, but the devil will edge us on to take it further and possibly sin. We can't let that happen if we profess to be practicing Christians. I'm apologizing because my innocent kiss on the cheek sparked a passion that could lead to temptation."

He twisted his kissable lips like a schoolboy, contemplating the correct answer to avoid getting in trouble. Taking her hands in his, Landon squeezed. "I can be modest in my affection with my woman." He lifted his brow in a challenge.

What? "Your woman? Since when?"

"Since the day at that Chinese performance, I have watched how certain scenes enthralled you, and I wanted to get to know you and share other experiences with you. It kept building."

Being with him was like a sweet fragrance that she couldn't sniff enough. "If I'm your woman, then you agree to respecting and protecting my reputation as a Christian woman. This is important to me."

"And me." He lifted her chin and inched closer as if he were going to kiss her, smiled, and then stepped back. "You have my word."

"Thank you." Gina returned to her desk to file away papers and tidy her area. There was no normalcy yet. There would be a mad rush from those who needed to file extensions, but her dad would return in a week, and they could handle that.

Landon sat, and she could feel him tracking her every mood. He said nothing to distract her, but after that brief kiss, she was flustered. Landon flirted and blew her kisses whenever she made eye contact with him.

Blushing, Gina fussed, "Will you stop that?"

Landon never answered her as she finished up. She liked everything about Landon—his looks, generous spirit to give back to the community, and commitment to Christ, which helped restrain him toward his woman.

His woman, she mused. It had been a while since she had been any man's plus one. Gina liked being someone's lady again.

Chapter Nine

With some breathing room the next day at work, Gina put more effort into finding the perfect unique ornament—a Black angel—to make Landon's grandmother happy.

She called Melody Ransom, the administrator at the children's home and the quality assurance gatekeeper for auction items. "I need a favor, and I know it's early, but could the children start on their Christmas projects? I understand we usually wait until summer break, but the woman who enjoys them is battling dementia. Her grandson wants her to experience the joy of Christmas while her mind is still stable."

"I'll do my best. Our little artisans are perfectionists anyway, so it might take a few weeks."

"Thanks." Gina ended the call and reflected on the canvas angel Landon had purchased at the highest price Denise could get. Although his Granny Lonna liked it, she wanted an ornament.

Denise knew their company didn't even sell the merchandise here because of a conflict of interest. The snack bar, yes, in conjunction with the Round-Up program, but Gina left that up to the charity manager when it came to the big moneymakers. Christmas Tax Help for All Seasons only got a sneak peek at the items.

Next, she called Leslie Littles, the foundation's manager, to request a list of contributors over the past five years.

If Gina could find out what the woman purchased in the past, she could ask that artisan to create a unique piece.

As she was set to lock up the office, Landon walked in the door.

Gina's smile blossomed. The man's shirts and pants were crisp. He had to own hundreds of ties. "Hey. What are you doing here?"

"Are you complaining?" he teased, towering over her with a wiggle of his eyebrow.

"Never." She walked into his arms for a hug. When she stepped back, he took her hand and twirled her under his arm. Throwing her head back, Gina laughed until he stopped. "Seriously, what are you doing here? I'm not working late anymore, and it's still light outside."

"Woman, you're a hard habit to break."

Landon made it hard for Gina not to reward him with another hug. With every touch, her senses came alive. She had to look away to avoid carrying out more affection.

"To answer your question, when I was thinking about you today, Granny Lonna came to mind, and—"

"I was thinking about her too." Gina didn't hide her surprise.

He patted his chest and then pointed to hers. "Our hearts are in sync. I want you to meet my grandmother."

Gina squeezed her lips in trepidation. "But I don't have a Black angel for her yet."

"It's not about the ornament. It's about you and me."

"O–Okay." Gina grabbed her purse, set the alarm, turned off the light, and stepped outside the door with Landon.

She hoped his grandmother liked her.

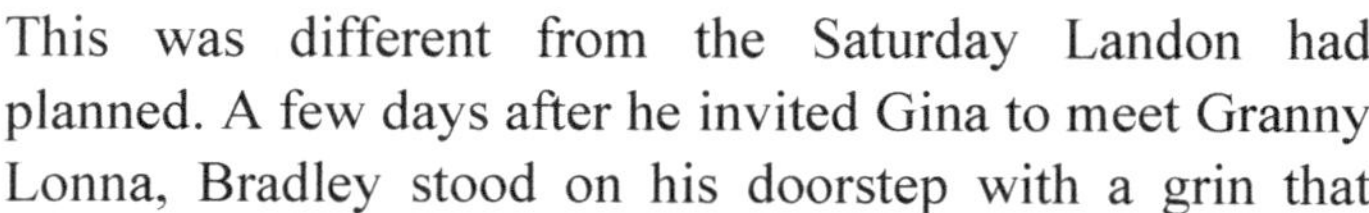

This was different from the Saturday Landon had planned. A few days after he invited Gina to meet Granny Lonna, Bradley stood on his doorstep with a grin that made Landon brace for his neighbor's shenanigans.

"I got a B-minus in pre-calculus. This cute girl, Nikki, tutored me after school."

They exchanged a high-five, and then Landon dropped his hands when Bradley suggested a double date. That's where Landon drew the line.

"Okay, okay." Bradley's grin widened. "I won two tickets for this Saturday from a contest off of social media, so I'm treating you this time."

How could Landon tell the young man he had mentored that he had a date that superseded everything else? He couldn't. Landon had worked hard to get Bradley to open up and trust him. Bradley's love of soccer was the key to earning higher grades. That meant missing out on time with Gina and his grandmother. Before he met Gina, nothing stood in the way of his mentorship…until now.

She was understanding when he told Gina that his plans were thwarted because of another soccer game.

"I don't know if City SC is one of Denise's clients, but I'm sure she can get some free tickets."

"No, we're good." He then explained how Bradley won them. Landon wanted to ask her to come to the game with them, but this was Bradley's escape from reality. When his mother gave him up, his grandmother took him in, and the teenager's future mattered to Landon.

On the day of the game, Landon put his personal life on hold and concentrated on Bradley's individual development.

The tickets gave them free admission to the stadium, but Landon treated Bradley to food and a pair of red-and-black sunglasses with the team's emblem. The pair settled in their seats and waited for the players to take the field.

"Are you still seeing the Christmas lady?" Bradley's unexpected question hung in the air.

"I am." Landon stared ahead. He didn't want to encourage more conversation about his personal life.

It worked. Bradley became animated with his play-by-play. Landon's entertainment was distracted when Gina texted him.

Miss you. Denise is boring compared to you. :) Enjoy your time with Bradley.

Landon chuckled, then grinned. He was glad she was thinking of him while they were apart.

"Must be the Christmas lady." Bradley shoved him. "You should have brought her."

"Don't I know it." Landon bit his bottom lip as he texted her back. **Miss you more.**

Chapter Ten

"You know I'm not going to live forever," Granny Lonna said while Landon prepared coffee, toast, and scrambled eggs for them in her small but modestly decorated mint green kitchen with black accents.

Granny Lonna was a petite woman with cinnamon-colored skin and had no deep-set wrinkles. Her skin was always soft and warm, as was her smile. This morning, her smile was absent, replaced by concern.

The previous night, he had dreamed she said those words *can't live forever*. Those haunting words woke him, and he couldn't force himself back to sleep.

So here he was, early on a Saturday morning, his heart heavy with worry, at his grandmother's place to convince himself that everything was alright. It had only been a meaningless dream.

After last week's soccer game with Bradley, Landon had hoped to pamper Gina with a show-and-tell Saturday to convey how much his feelings had progressed in a short period. He had planned to treat her to a mid-morning spa, lunch, and dinner and tell Gina he loved her.

Already, his plans had changed.

Thinking about Gina took Landon's mind off Granny Lonna, but her condition and request couldn't be ignored, especially when his grandmother was direct like this.

Granny Lonna was speaking to him, and he had zoned out.

"I don't want to talk about it all the time," Landon said, adding a slight trace of sugar to the coffee, which was more cream, and then placing the cup in front of her.

"I have a bucket list." She grinned before taking a sip.

At eighty-two, what hadn't his grandmother accomplished that she was still clinging to her last breath to fulfill?

"I want to see another generation of great-grands. You and Janay need to ask the Lord to help you find love. I want to see you both happy."

Landon smiled. "Look at me, Granny Lonna. I am happy."

She peered through her glasses and studied him, then grunted. "Prove it."

The doorbell rang, then a key turned the lock. Seconds later, his only sibling stood in the doorway with carryout. She visited every other weekend since she lived in Kansas City.

"Hey." Janay's eyes were bright with shock. "What are you doing here on a Saturday?"

Did she have a dream that caused her to come early, too? Landon wasn't about to ask a question that might confirm his dream wasn't random. "I came to check on my sweet grandmother."

Janay leaned over and placed a loud, juicy kiss on her cheek.

Granny Lonna beamed, then pushed the breakfast he'd prepared to the side and reached for Janay's bag.

He feigned insult and frowned. "Hey, you told me what you had a taste for, and that's what I cooked." He didn't have an appetite until his sister strolled in with a bag of biscuits dusted with powdered sugar on the top. "Did you bring enough for your big brother?"

"I guess I can spare one," she teased, then placed the bag on the table and kissed Landon.

Since Granny Lonna's release from the hospital earlier in the year, his parents usually checked on her during the week between nurse visits. Janay visited on Saturdays, and Landon stopped by after church on Sundays.

Janay joined them at the table and blessed her food. After a few bites, Granny Lonna repeated her desire for great-grands.

"You should talk to your grandson. He's the one dating."

"O-ooh." His grandmother eyed him. "Why haven't I met her?"

"You will today." Landon stood and walked into the other room to make a private phone call. His plans for the day with Gina had to be tweaked. Hopefully, she wouldn't be disappointed.

Gina woke to Landon's ringtone. She smiled. "Morning."

"Good morning to you, too. I hope it's not too early."

Grinning, Gina stretched and eyed the time. "I'll never refuse your wake-up call."

"Thanks. Neither will I. Is today good for you to meet Granny Lonna?"

His voice was urgent, putting her on alert. "Sure. Is everything okay?"

Landon was quiet, and that scared her.

"Landon?" She scooted up in bed.

"Her condition worries me."

Awww. She wished she could hug him. "Will she fuss at me because the items she wants haven't come in yet? I've opened every box that's been delivered, whether from the children's home or individuals, in hopes it would be the one ornament your grandmother wants." She gnawed on her lips, which needed moisturizer.

"I know, baby."

"These creative minds are still in school. If they keep their grades up and stay out of trouble, they can work in the makeshift studio at the children's home once their homework is done. That's why we get a lot in the summer and early September…"

Wait. Gina's brain rewound. She sucked in her breath in hopes of ingesting the bliss that came from the endearment. "Landon?" Her heart pounded.

"Yes?"

"Did you call me baby?" Gina's heart swayed to a slow beat. "Was that intentional, or a slip of the tongue?"

He released a low chuckle, and his voice deepened. "Make no mistake about it. I said what I said, and I'm not taking it back."

Closing her eyes, Gina recorded the sound of his voice and his declaration in her head. This man liked to push her buttons with his challenges, so she didn't have time to respond without overthinking things.

"And I hope you're feeling some kind of way toward me, too."

"I am." But to say it meant surrendering her heart, but in a month was too soon for her.

"Well, I'll give you time to process what I said. I'll be at your house in a few hours to spend the day with Granny Lonna."

"I'll be ready." Gina ended the call and immediately phoned her sister.

Denise answered, "Wherever you want to drag me to, forget it and call Landon. I'm trying to sleep my Saturday away."

Gina laughed. "Thanks to you, Landon will take me wherever I want to go."

"So why are you waking me up?" Denise yawned.

"Because Landon called me baby." Gina gritted her teeth and contained her scream of delight as she kicked her legs under the covers. "And today, I'm going to meet his grandmother."

"Call me after you two share your first kiss. It's not even noon, so I'm going back to sleep."

No way would Gina kiss and tell that.

Gina smiled the whole time she got ready, recalling his term of endearment and looking forward to being with him today. Excitement had her waiting outside when Landon arrived with flowers. He got out and hurried toward her, and Gina melted in his arms—he was her happy place where she found contentment.

Their kiss was brief.

Their hug was longer.

When he released her, he asked, "You nervous?"

"A little." Gina took the flowers inside and returned minutes later as he waited, then they walked to his vehicle and slid into the passenger seat. "Thank your grandmother for sending you to our business."

He chuckled as he waited for her to click her seatbelt. "Yes, because there's no way I would have gone Christmas shopping in March without her urging." He made his way to his side of the car and got in.

Gina grinned. "Then my sister set us up. I would have forfeited those tickets if it hadn't been for *Shen Yun*, and she knew it."

"Something else I never would have attended without you." He reached over, slipped his fingers through hers, and then brought them to his lips. "Gina, you don't have to be shy about your feelings. Whenever you're ready to share, I'm ready."

"Thank you." Gina had been in a one-sided relationship before, and she felt unappreciated. That was the last thing she wanted Landon to experience. But she didn't want to rush. Gina wanted to make sure of the growing emotions Landon stirred in her. She knew no relationship was perfect, but she needed the right man with flaws and all who would be perfect for her.

Landon drove through a pair of wrought-iron gates that opened to one-story residences. The homes were picture-perfect, with small front lawns and blooming flowers racing around porches. Some had American flags hanging from columns on porches, while others had spring seasonal banners. A few residents had nothing at all.

"This is a nice senior living community," Gina said as they parked across the street in a designated visitor lot.

Landon walked around his vehicle, opened her door, then took her hand. His touch was gentle, and the look in his eyes tugged at her heartstrings as he tugged her out of his vehicle. "Come on. You'll love Granny Lonna."

He rang the doorbell and didn't wait to use his key to open the door. The fragrance of baked apples or gingerbread tickled their senses.

Each step Gina took drew her into the virtual home of Mr. and Mrs. Claus. Christmas decorations graced the fireplace's mantel, and five-foot nutcrackers were posted on each side. That was in the living room. Across the hall, a small dining room was transformed into a dollhouse with every kind of Black angel—from ornaments to tree toppers to art.

"Wow." Gina pointed and crossed the threshold into the room. "I remember that angel from our collection a few years ago." It was sentimental to see art appreciated regardless of the artisan's age. The pieces were mixed with more expensive holiday decor.

Before she could further investigate, a petite woman appeared, holding onto a young woman's arm—Landon's younger sister. The same age as Gina. "Hello."

"You must be Gina. It's nice to meet you finally. I'm Janay."

"My Black angel," Landon's grandmother said, walking closer with her finger extended, ready to touch to see if Gina was real.

"Oh no, Mrs. Williams, our yearly collection of Black angels, ornaments, and other Christmas items aren't available yet. It's a little early for our children to have finished anything." Gina smiled.

"No, dear. Call me Granny Lonna. My grandson has finally brought me the Black angel I wanted." Her eyes twinkled, and her face glowed excitedly as if Gina were a peppermint cane.

Confused, Gina looked at Landon, his sister, then back at his grandmother. Was Granny Lonna expecting Gina to have the angel in her possession?

"Granny Lonna," Janay said. "This is Landon's girlfriend, Gina Christmas."

The older woman looked at her knowingly. "More beautiful than I imagined. My Black angel," Granny Lonna repeated as her granddaughter guided her back to the kitchen.

What was going on? Was the woman hallucinating? Gina touched his arm. "Are you okay?"

"Yeah." He swallowed but kept his focus on the direction of his grandmother.

"Ah, do you think she thinks I'm an angel?" she whispered. If so, Gina was too late to help Landon find the ornament to celebrate Christmas eight months early while her mind was still in the present.

She never got her answer as he tugged her toward the kitchen. Landon was quiet. What was he thinking? Gina had no one-on-one experience with a loved one living with dementia, so she didn't know what Granny Lonna's normal behavior was.

They sat at the table with a platter of fried chicken drumettes and other finger foods. Landon took his grandmother's hand and gave her his attention. It was as if everything, including Gina, faded into the background.

Landon didn't take his eyes off Granny Lonna as he communicated to her with a smile. Gina exchanged glances with his sister, whose eyes were glazed over.

This was a private moment. Gina didn't belong in it. Plus, her appetite suddenly vanished, so she could do nothing to distract herself.

"Granny Lonna," Landon's voice seemed to coo with its gentle tone, "Gina is not an angel. She's my beautiful girlfriend."

The woman laughed, swatting his arm. "I know that. I want an angel as beautiful as her."

The three of them seemed to exhale from her admission. *Whew*. Gina blushed.

"You two would make pretty babies, then I would be a great-grandmother and have tea parties with my great-grandchildren. The little boys I would let loose in the backyard like I did you." She pointed to Landon. "She reminds me of the beautiful Black angels I got from the Christmas Shoppe. Is George your grandfather?"

"Why, yes." Gina's heart raced, inching closer to the edge of her seat to hear every word. It had been some time since she met someone who knew her grandfather.

"He was kind to my late husband—and me. They often called each other brothers, but that was long ago." She shivered and reached for a plate. "Landon, give thanks for our food. We haven't eaten since yesterday."

Gina blinked in surprise and mumbled, "Yesterday?"

Landon and Janay shook their heads in denial and sadness.

He took Gina's hand and squeezed as they all joined hands. Once he gave thanks, Gina's appetite returned as she listened to stories about the Michaels family.

Janay munched and said, "Gina, I'm glad I was here when Landon brought you to see Granny Lonna, or there's no telling if we ever would have met."

"Stop it." Landon grunted at his sister. "We're all working professionals who are busy."

"Gina, you and I will have to plan to do something together one day," Janay said. She worked in telemedicine, having double majored in computer science and premed. Shy about her impressive accomplishments, Landon didn't hold back his adoration of his younger sister.

"Yes, and I'll invite my sister, Denise, to join us."

"Yeah, the little matchmaker," Landon mumbled, then smiled at Janay. "My baby's passionate, a force to be reckoned with when it comes to forensic accounting."

So Landon had been listening during one of their long chats when she mentioned some clients had suspected embezzlement, and Gina had billed them top dollar to uncover the layers of thievery. It wasn't about the money, but the crime, the layers of deceit, which were time-consuming.

Granny Lonna's eyes twinkled with pride as she listened to the young folks' accomplishments.

A couple of hours passed when Landon stood and stretched, then pulled Gina to her feet. "Granny Lonna, it's time for us to leave." He hugged her, then Gina did the same, soaking up the older woman's warm embrace. Gina was in no rush, entertained by the family stories.

"It was so nice meeting you."

"And you too, dear."

As she and Landon walked to the door, they overheard the older woman tell her granddaughter, "I told you she was a Black angel."

Landon's hand stiffened. *Why?* She wondered about his reaction.

Hoping to get an answer didn't happen. He remained quiet on the ride back to her house. Landon escorted her to the door. She placed her hands on his clean-shaven cheeks, and they shared a soft kiss.

"I'll make sure I save the most beautiful ornament for Granny Lonna."

"It may not matter. We already might be too late." Landon huffed and jogged down the stairs without looking back.

Chapter Eleven

Landon had hoped his day with Gina would have gone differently. He wanted to profess his love, but hearing Granny Lonna's odd conversation made him backtrack. Loving someone hurts too much.

After he dropped her off, he went home to sit in the dark and, honestly, let depression keep him company.

Gina's ringtone lit up Landon's phone screen. She left a message. Persistent, she texted him: **Are you alright?**

Childishly, he ignored both.

Although he cared about her, Landon didn't want her to see him in a bad mood.

If Landon had known Granny Lonna would have responded oddly, he would not have invited Gina to witness it.

Landon's heart was breaking. When would Granny Lonna no longer know him, Janay, or his parents? He wasn't prepared for that. His thoughts were too jumbled to talk. He reread the text. Was he okay? Rubbing his face, Landon shook his head.

Suddenly, this seemed like the wrong time for a relationship. Gina might come to that conclusion too. There was something special about Gina, but Landon wasn't in the right head space to give her all of him. He stared at the phone, counting time by the tick of the wall clock. Landon exhaled, then played her message.

Hi, Landon. I know you weren't the same man who dropped me off as the one who picked me up today. I know you care about me and Granny Lonna, or we would've never crossed paths. I'm here for you. Let me hold your hand through this journey. I don't have answers or might not know what to say, but I'd rather you know I'm here. Save me a seat tomorrow at your church. I'm coming and will continue to be there for you as you were for me at the office every evening when my dad was out. I can't let you go through this uncertainty alone. Good night, baby.

In case you didn't hear me, I called you baby. She giggled, then the message ended.

The darkness of depression that tried to engulf him began to dissipate. Landon tapped her name to hear her voice.

And she would hear the sadness in his. Landon shook his head. "Can't."

He reached for the remote to turn on the light and stared at his surroundings—a three-bedroom house that seemed to swallow him up at the moment.

Landon sent Gina a text: **Sorry for my behavior. You deserved a better man. I wasn't him today. Tomorrow is Easter. Wouldn't you rather be with your family at your church?**

Her offer touched him, whether she came or not, to know she was willing spoke volumes of her feelings that she hadn't whispered.

Yes, but I can worship the Lord with you. Whether you admit it or not, you like me.

Landon laughed until a tear dropped. *This is the woman I want*. He grinned as he responded. **I'll pick you up so you can hold my hand. :)**

Seconds later, she replied with hearts that ascended in the air. **I'll be ready at ten.**

Gina made no other demands on him that night, including "Let's talk." He was grateful for that. It was as if she knew he needed space.

As he prepared for bed, Landon felt free to pray, cry out to the Lord, and tell Him about his pain. "Jesus, I'm scared. I know Your Word says to be absent in the body is to be present with the Lord, but what happens until then?" He needed his grandmother's mind to stay current with her body.

As tears trickled down his face, Landon felt the presence of God.

I will never leave you or your grandmother, God whispered. *I'm a very present help in times of trouble.*

God gave him comfort, and so did Gina. Landon whispered, "In Jesus' name. Amen."

It wasn't the day Landon had hoped, but he and Gina became closer than planned.

The following day, Landon was in a better mood. The prayer the night before had refreshed him. He called Gina to confirm that she was attending his church instead of hers.

"I'm ready and enjoying a cup of coffee." Gina dragged out a sip to prove it, making him laugh. "I'm glad to hear your voice," she said softly.

Landon closed his eyes. All he wanted now was for Gina to talk to him, encourage him, and tell him she loved him…if she did. But he could wait.

They ended the call, and Landon dressed in record time. When he arrived at her house, she was standing on the porch. She stepped down, all smiles. Seeing Gina made everything alright in his world.

Kingdom Come Church—Landon's church—was half an hour from Gina's house.

The congregation was less than a thousand people, and the age group was diverse. When the couple entered the sanctuary, a minister stood at the podium, offering the morning prayer.

The praise singers belted out contemporary worship songs. Landon stood and stretched out his hands in surrender. Gina stood by his side.

When his parents and sister arrived at his pew, Landon introduced his parents to Gina. Janay hugged Gina, and so did his mother, Rhonda, who didn't want to let Gina go. When his family sat, his mother leaned across Janay and asked her questions.

Why did his mother want to chat with Gina now? Landon reminded them that service was underway.

"Sorry," Rhonda Michaels apologized. "Maybe we can talk after service."

There was no way Landon was about to let his busy bee mother monopolize Gina's time. He needed his lady today more than them.

When Pastor Andy Kilroy stepped to the podium to greet the congregation and welcome guests, Gina stood to be acknowledged along with other visitors and received hearty applause. His mother's clap was the loudest.

Landon admired Gina from head to toe—again. *Nice.* He was in selfish mode from the soft green dress that fitted her waist, complemented by organza sleeves and beige shoes that supported her shapely legs. He didn't plan to share her with his parents.

When she took her seat, Gina slipped her fingers through his, and he tugged her closer until their shoulders touched. The spark he felt seemed to recharge every emotion he felt for her.

"Happy Resurrection, saints and friends. If you have your Bible, turn to John fifteen verse thirteen. '*Greater love hath no man than this, that a man lay down his life for his friends.*' I'm talking about Jesus today. We weren't always friends of God. Sin separated us and made us the Lord's archenemy, but praise God, through the washing of His blood and receiving His Spirit, we are worthy to be called His friends…"

The message was comforting, empowering, and inspiring. Landon was glad Gina had sacrificed her service to attend his. He had to tell her how he felt.

Pastor Kilroy closed his Bible half an hour after a fiery sermon about the power of the resurrection: "Repent, friends. The blood Jesus shed on the cross thousands of years ago still works and can wash your sins away. Jesus Christ got up from the grave, and so can you on the day of His re-appearing, which we call the rapture of His church. Will you come?"

A few did. More followed until the altar was packed with men, women, and children who repented of their sins and wanted to be saved through the baptism of water and spirit.

Landon turned to Gina. Her eyes were misty. "Are you okay?"

Sniffling, she nodded. "This is the emotional part of the service for me…to know that people are repenting and bypassing hell." Patting her chest, she was choked with an emotion he had never witnessed before, as if she knew the folks personally.

Landon squeezed her hand, although he wanted to hug her tight and never let go.

Two ministers entered the pool, which was the backdrop behind the pulpit. Lights flashed, and the sound of water echoed throughout the sanctuary. Candidates dressed in white clothes stepped into the water from the other side. One woman wore a swim cap, and the other had her braids tied back.

The ministers had them cross their hands over their chests. Each minister rested one hand on their back and lifted the other hand.

"My dear sisters, upon the confession of your faith and the repentance in your hearts, we now indeed baptize in you in the mighty name of our Lord and Savior Jesus Christ, for there is no other name under heaven by which we must be saved, for the remission of your sins in Jesus' name. And you shall receive the promise of the Holy Ghost with the evidence of speaking with heavenly tongues, in Jesus' name. Amen."

Gina leaped from her seat and worshipped Jesus, along with others. She praised God as if the candidate was her own family.

Landon was touched and stood, too. From the corner of his eye, he noticed Gina's expression was of awe.

By the end of the service, countless other candidates were baptized in Jesus' name. Gina fanned herself. She appeared more exhausted than fans at a soccer game.

"Whew." Gina grinned, then hugged him. Before he could latch on to her, she turned and hugged Janay, his mother, again and waved at his father.

Love was in the air. Not only God's love but the love Landon had for Gina.

Gina mused at Easter service about what love feels like—God's love and the gift He gave for couples to find a special someone.

Although the Michaelses begged Gina to join them for dinner, Landon wouldn't concede.

"She's mine today, fam," he said with finality.

And Gina didn't protest. She was worried about him emotionally and wanted to make sure he was coping and not putting on a façade.

Once they were in his SUV, Gina waited for him to drive off, but he didn't immediately. "Landon?"

He turned and gave her his full attention. "Yeah, baby?"

"I'm hungry."

Looking away, Landon stalled for an answer, then faced her. "Brunch? I want it to be you and me—no family today. Okay?"

Gina covered his free hand with both of hers. "Of course."

On the way to Brewster's House for brunch, Gina was quiet. She wanted to be a sounding board to whatever he wanted to talk about.

Five minutes into the ride, Landon glanced at her. "Yesterday, I had planned to treat you to a spa, lunch, and dinner…"

Really? Gina didn't attempt to hide her surprise.

"The purpose was to show and tell you that I love everything about you—even our differences in our approach to charity are negotiable."

Humph. Not really. However, she said nothing.

"Since yesterday was a bust to show you, it doesn't stop me from telling you that I love you, Gina." He looked back at the road and continued. "You've displayed how much you care and love me by coming to me, so…"

They stopped at a light, and he turned to face her.

"Baby, when are you going to tell me?"

Gina smiled. It was time to put him out of his mental torment. Landon had enough on his mind. "Landon Michaels, I love you, and I'm not so sure we can change each other's mind on how to give back, but this moment is about letting you know I got your back."

She giggled when Landon straightened in his seat and flashed her the biggest smile for the rest of the way.

At Brewster's House, they filled their plates in the brunch line. Gina chose a table that gave them some privacy in the busy restaurant. They sat, and Gina watched him pray. "Jesus, I don't have the words to convey my thanks for Your Resurrection, our families, especially Granny Lonna and Gina. I love her, and You allowed us to be together and share this meal. Please sanctify it from all impurities, and let us never forget to pray and pay it forward in Jesus' name. Amen."

Gina looked up first and watched him lift his head. His handsomeness was a distraction and so were his mesmerizing eyes.

"What?"

"Oh, nothing." She tilted her head. "I just love a man who prays."

Their Resurrection Day ended with comforting hugs, warm, sweet kisses, and whispers of love.

Chapter Twelve

Gina watched her father stroll into the office like a visitor after a few unexpected recovery setbacks two weeks past the tax season deadline. He scanned the lobby from left to right.

Welcome back balloons were tied to the back of his office chair, which could be seen with the blinds pulled to the top. Gina stood and hugged her dad tight.

Ray strolled to the short hall into his office and settled in his chair, and she trailed him. He patted the top of his desk, which Gina had tidied after April 15, and sighed. "*Ahhh*, it feels good to be back. Sorry to leave you in a bind, but you handled things easily and met a nice young man. Maybe I'll retire early."

"Don't you dare!" Gina straightened from leaning against his office doorway. "Dad, it was anything but easy. We already had a lot of existing clients, so I had to turn away walk-ins, which meant we lost revenue. I think we need to bring in an intern or hire a part-time accounting clerk for next tax season."

When her desk phone rang, Gina hurried to the front to answer it.

"Gina, this is Leslie. I've sent you a list of people who purchased from the charity. Check your email."

"Will do. Thanks." Gina ended the call and logged into her email. She opened the Excel file from Leslie. She did a quick scan, and there was no record of Lonna Williams as a donor, only three Donna Williamses. Was Lonna her real name? Gina twisted her mouth, thinking. "*Hmmm.* Or it could be a typo in the system." Two Donnas lived out of state. She called the foundation manager back. "Hey, Leslie, will you send me an image of what Donna Williams from St. Louis purchased?"

"Hold on." She typed on her keyboard.

Seconds later, Gina opened the new email and clicked on the attachment. She studied the photo while Leslie was on the line. It could be the same piece Gina had seen in Granny Lonna's house.

"Leslie, I think this is the same person, but the address doesn't match the one I visited. Thanks for helping." She ended the call and texted Landon to verify his grandmother's previous address.

Hi, baby. Your grandmother's name is Lonna, not Donna, right? Before she lived in the senior community, was her address 4052 Westline Street? I'm trying to find an angel match.

Landon verified that this was the correct information. She texted him back: **Thanks. Hugs and kisses.**

I only accept those in person, love.

Gina giggled. **Noted.**

Next, she called Leslie and asked her to correct the first name and update the new mailing address. "I also saw two other pieces that seemed familiar and I wonder if those came from our children too."

"It would be tedious, but if you can get a picture of them and send it to me, I can cross reference to see who purchased them because Lonna Williams did not."

"*Hmmm*. Okay, thanks." Gnawing on her lips, Gina's suspicious nature kicked in. They once had a volunteer who was caught stealing and reselling items. The woman was banned from the charity, but that was so long ago. That wasn't the case now. Maybe they were a gift. She needed to take pictures.

Would Landon become suspicious about her charities' books not being balanced or missing inventory because she couldn't track an item?

Gina pushed her concern to the back of her mind so that she could perform her day job. Four quarterly reports awaited her attention by the end of the month. Gina didn't need any more distractions. She focused so she didn't have to work overtime.

May began as the prelude to summer fun. Food festivals, including the annual Taste of Maplewood Street Festival, would start popping up across the city—a treat she couldn't wait to share with Landon.

An hour into an unproductive morning, a deliveryman walked through the door with a bouquet of spring flowers. She thanked the man, then sniffed as her father strolled out of his office.

"Are you and Landon serious?" Ray folded his arms and leaned against a wall. He wasn't going to leave until she answered.

Gina turned around and looked into his eyes. "I like spending time with him and miss him when we're not together. He's open to exploring events with me…and we admitted our love to each other."

"But?" Her father lifted a brow.

"We don't see eye to eye on *everything*. The man has a stubborn side when it comes to charities' accountabilities. I feel a certain way about that."

Squinting, he pointed to the flowers. "Denise thinks he's a perfect match for you, and I agree, considering he came every evening during tax season to make sure you were safe. Whatever kinks you two are facing will work themselves out." He smiled and returned to his office.

At about one in the afternoon, Landon walked through the door with to-go Styrofoam containers. He greeted her with a sweet, short kiss, mindful that her dad was in the building.

"Thank you for the flowers." She tried to sound upbeat, but maybe it was overkill. She needed to take a closer look at his grandmother's angels.

Her dad reappeared, and Landon walked to him with an extended hand. "Mr. Christmas, welcome back. I'm glad Gina isn't here alone anymore."

"You ensured she wasn't, and I appreciate you keeping her safe."

"It was my pleasure. I brought enough lunch for the three of us." He took the containers out of the bag and placed them on a side table near the nook while Gina retrieved plates, napkins, and utensils from the small back kitchen.

As the trio chatted, the door opened, and Melody struggled with a medium-sized box from the children's home. Landon jumped up and immediately relieved her of the load.

"Goody. What do you have for me?" Grinning, Gina hoped there was something inside that Granny Lonna would like.

"About twelve pieces. Our little creators have been busy, and I can't believe their skill level, considering many of them are self-taught." She smiled proudly.

"They are God-inspired," Gina said. "Please tell the children thank you. Hopefully, those pieces will sell fast."

"I will. The uniforms came in for the parade. They are so cute. You will be there, right?" Melody asked.

Proceeds from the Round-Up program were used to meet children's other miscellaneous needs. Pocket change adds up when purchases are rounded up to the nearest dollar.

"Of course. Cheering them on. Sorry for my bad manners. This is Landon, my boyfriend, and we'll be there."

Landon smiled and shook her hand.

Melody gave him an appreciative nod, then left minutes later. Her father returned to his office with his plate of fish, spaghetti, and potato salad from one of the best chicken and fish places in Midtown.

"Come on. Don't you want to see what's inside? You seem distracted," Landon said as he wiped his hands and mouth.

"Sure. Let me get the scissors." Gina pulled out eight pieces to be used for the auction. "Wow."

Landon's jaw dropped as Gina admired each piece. "These are incredible."

"I know, right?" Gina grinned but hid her disappointment that none were the Black angels she had hoped the children would make. If so, Gina would have set it aside and made an exception for Landon to purchase it.

"I wouldn't mind buying the mother and child figurine made from wire for my mom for Mother's Day," Landon said.

Gina groaned within. Great. She was about to become what she disliked—a rule breaker if it had been a Black angel and now a hypocrite because she was about to change the rules.

"Sorry." Gina shook her head. "Can't sell them now. We let the older children participate in the Christmas in July auction because the monies go into a trust fund for the children for college. The other Christmas items are for sale for holiday gifts, and that money goes into the general fund to be used throughout the year for requests that come in."

"You're amazing. I know I can't bribe you to change your mind about the figurine." Landon held her hands. "I gave you a hard time when we first met, but I see my baby knows what she is doing and is honest."

Gina couldn't accept the accolades. She needed to repent, and she did.

"I better get back to work. Let's plan a mid-week dinner, okay?" Landon said.

"I would like that."

They stole a kiss, and Landon was gone.

Taking out her laptop, Gina's heart dropped. Not even the flowers could make her smile for long as she flopped in the chair and emailed Leslie about the impressive new items. She sighed as she sent the message to pick them up anytime.

She called Denise and told her about the items she saw at Landon's grandmother's house. "I believe at least three of the items were made by our children at the home, and only one shows Granny Lonna purchasing it. The name is listed as Donna instead of Lonna. I need to get a photo of them to cross-reference in our database."

"That's simple. Have Landon take a photo. Problem solved," Denise said. "You're definitely overthink things."

"Maybe, but he wouldn't know which ones, and I don't want to hint that I'm concerned about missing inventory." Gina sighed and scratched her head as she ended the call with her sister. Maybe she was overthinking things. No one would dare steal from children, right? It happened before.

Chapter Thirteen

It seemed like a lifetime ago when Landon would leave his Clayton office and drive downtown to Gina's to stay with her until she was ready to go home.

Landon missed those two weeks when it was just them, and he would watch her work. She was intense and beautiful. It was bittersweet because he missed ending his evenings walking Gina to her car now that Mr. Christmas was back on the job.

The timing was perfect because a few projects on his job became more demanding. One day, he spent most of his time on a site near his parents' house, so he visited them.

His mother had warmed up leftovers and prepared him a plate. His father blessed their meal. Landon got an update on his grandmother's condition.

"Granny Lonna has her moments when she's in the present with us, and then other times, she seems to struggle with brain fog," Rhonda advised him. "The doctors say to be patient and not force her memories—it will only agitate her."

As long as his grandmother's episodes didn't seem to be worsening, there was still hope to get the ornament she wanted and celebrate Christmas, regardless of the date on the calendar.

"That's why we have to live every day and not worry about tomorrow," his father said.

Landon nodded. "Gina's pastor preached something like that last week: 'Work While It's Daylight,' taken from John nine verse four. I like her pastor's preaching."

His mother smiled. "I like Gina. She's such a sweetheart. You make a nice-looking and loving couple."

Grinning, Landon swallowed his food. "Thanks, Mom. She's special."

"We see that." His father chuckled.

"You two alternating between her church and ours each Sunday is a good idea," his mother said, then added, "You look like a family man."

"Mom, stop digging. Gina and I are on our own timeline."

Landon couldn't be happier. He was glad he had told Gina how he felt. The trust between them was growing. He had met the love of his life, and since Easter, he and Gina had started alternating church visits. This Sunday, he would attend Christ Has Risen Church. Landon was as comfortable there as Gina was at his church.

One misconception Landon had was about accountants. Landon assumed Gina's workload would be light since tax season was over. She worked late a couple of times this week, but her father was with her. It was for the best, as he monitored Granny Lonna more closely and didn't have to worry about Gina.

With the weekend approaching, Landon had another commitment. As part of his mentorship to young black and brown boys, Landon and other professionals volunteered once a month to engage youths and keep them off the streets on Friday nights. This was his week to shoot hoops from ten until midnight.

Gina wasn't into sports, so he didn't know if his lady would opt out of this date. Bradley had never been interested since it wasn't soccer.

"I didn't know you were athletic. I thought you were just a gym rat. Sure, I'll be your cheerleader," she told him over the phone from her office.

"And the prettiest one." Landon was hyped.

She deserved every compliment he gave her. Gina was the package deal—looks, genuine personality, and spiritual walk. Like him, she was a practicing Christian who kept him on the straight and narrow whenever they were passionate. Plus, Granny Lonna's eyes lit up whenever Landon took Gina to visit her.

"Let me see if I can drag Denise to come along."

Landon released a hearty laugh but had to temper himself at work. "Sorry, babe. Don't be surprised if her answer is no. She dumped those tickets on me out of desperation to avoid attending the Chinese performance, but it was the best blessing for me."

"But I won't know anyone there, and you'll be on the court, probably losing badly while I'm alone in the stands," she teased.

Landon grunted. He wished they weren't on the phone in their respective offices. "Number one, I can play. Thirty-five is not old. I know the other ladies will make you feel welcome. I've got to go, baby." He hurried to end the call to review his notes with the project manager.

That evening, when Landon arrived at Gina's house, she looked youthful in the doorway with her jeans, tennis shoes, and an HBCU T-shirt. Her long, natural hair was swept up into a ponytail. The only makeup he could see was a gloss over her lips. He hated having to share her attention tonight with others at the game.

Although Landon was a kisser, Gina preferred hugs, and sometimes, they could hold each other so gently that a few times, Landon thought she had fallen asleep. "I wish I could skip tonight and take you out." Landon was halfway serious; if Gina hinted she didn't want to go, that would be good enough of an excuse for him to be a no-show.

Her teasing smile made Landon wonder at her thoughts. "Landon, that's not you. I've never met a man so committed to his convictions." She tugged at her oversized tote bag, pulled out pom-poms, and grinned. "Ready?"

Shaking his head, Landon laughed. "My woman. Come on, #TeamLandon, let's go." Linking his fingers through hers, he led her to his vehicle.

Twenty minutes later, when he and Gina walked through Wohl Center's doors to the gym, holding hands, Landon braced himself for his friends' ribbing.

Jay, Reggie, and Carlo were fellow Black engineers from different companies.

"This is Gina Christmas, an—" Landon paused. "She's my lady, so don't even think about making holiday jokes about her last name."

"You mean about the other women you've brought to the games?" Jay smirked. He was a talented engineer but messy when it came to relationships.

Reggie popped him in the stomach. "Man, you better cool it."

Landon squinted at Jay, then continued with Gina to the bleachers. "I will fight that man over you."

"No, you won't. As a Christian, you're not going to take the bait."

Gina meant everything to him. *Sometimes, I'd rather take the bait*, Landon thought as he walked away, praying he wouldn't have to do that.

Chapter Fourteen

Gina sensed the tension between Landon and Jay, thick like a slice of dry cake. Men and their hormones. It wouldn't do good for the adults to get into it.

From what Landon told her, the professionals engaged the youths to build character, confidence, and conflict resolution and to pique their interest in STEM programs.

The other ladies were friendly, and as expected, they commented on her last name, which always opened the door for her to witness for the Lord. "My family carries our last name with a badge of honor."

"Well, if you and Landon get married, you get to ditch the name," Misty, Jay's lady friend, said.

"I like my surname." Gina didn't say more. Since she didn't know them, Gina wouldn't drop morsels of information about her relationship to a group for gossip material.

Even though her sister didn't come with her, Gina hadn't had as much fun at a sports game since her older brother was in high school. "I didn't sign up for attending sporting events," Denise quipped when Gina extended the invite to the Friday night youth and adult basketball game. "Shopping, lunch, or spa—sign me up. Sports—clock me out."

Landon was her world now, and she wanted to support him as he had been there for her during the latter part of tax season.

Denise joked about momma's claws coming out. She hoped she wouldn't need girlfriend claws. Gina didn't. the night ended on cordial goodbyes.

That Sunday, on Mother's Day, Denise and Gina smothered their mother with breakfast at home, flowers, a nice dinner at an expensive restaurant, and there was a three-hundred-dollar gift card from their brother. Landon also spent the day with his mother and grandmother to celebrate Mother's Day. He still sent her three texts, reminding her that he missed her.

Next weekend, it's about us. Landon.

The following Sunday after service, Landon and Gina changed into something more casual, wearing matching denim and yellowish-gold shirts—a jumper for her and shorts for him.

Landon couldn't stop staring at his lady as they drove downtown for the Annie Malone parade, the spring highlight for African Americans in St. Louis. Gina glowed with excitement.

Her smile made him smile. When Gina faced him, she asked, "What?"

Landon chuckled. "Oh, I just love you and like seeing you happy."

"*Awww*, I love you, too." She covered his hand. "The Annie Malone parade never gets old to me. I'm glad to know that for more than a hundred years, it has reached the status of the second-largest African-American parade in the country to celebrate the Black pioneer who helped so many. Every Day is Christmas charity purchased sixteen uniforms for cheerleaders for the event. I can't wait to see the girls. They worked hard on their grades to earn them."

"I'm excited because you're excited. I've volunteered with the organization throughout the years."

Gina nodded. "I just don't have that type of time. Instead, I created the Every Day is Christmas charity five years ago to support the children's home twice a year. On a smaller scale, some local downtown businesses participate in our Round-Up program with snack boxes, too."

"You are amazing." He squeezed her hand, brought it to his lips, and kissed it. Gina's hand lotion was as intoxicating as her beauty, and Landon was addicted.

Landon found a parking spot a distance away and was glad Gina had changed from her heels into comfy walking shoes, knowing they were coming to the parade.

Families and spectators had started to gather along the parade route. He slipped his fingers through Gina's and kept her close to his side, passing food vendors and merchandise kiosks.

Both saw random friends and clients they knew, and he and Gina introduced themselves. Landon felt Gina's excitement as she waited for the group her charity had sponsored uniforms for to strut down Market Street.

A trail of convertibles from the St. Louis Corvette Club drove media personalities and other local celebrities. The parade had it all: marching bands, high-steppers, and floats. This was a major fundraiser for Annie Malone Children's Home and a not-to-be-missed event in St. Louis.

Finally, Gina grinned and pointed. "Ooh. That's them. They look so cute. My babies," she gushed and clapped loudly as young girls began cheers and gymnastics for the onlookers.

"I never imagined coming to the parade without bringing my children," he said, gauging her thoughts on motherhood.

"I want children, Landon." Gina beamed, then whipped her head back to the parade.

"Good to know." He hugged her. Gina Christmas was the one.

No blemishes.

She checked all his boxes with brains and beauty.

Chapter Fifteen

Gina massaged her forehead with her fingers. She didn't have a headache, but would if she continued stressing about the Black angels for Landon's grandmother.

Denise had suggested some covert activity to either get Landon's grandmother out of the house or to go in with a body camera. Gina had to laugh at that one because her sister was a mystery show fanatic.

Whenever Gina asked Landon about Granny Lonna, his response was "about the same." He never mentioned another visit.

Gina had prayed diligently for three days about what to do next to ease her worry, but no word had come from the Lord.

So now she had to take matters into her own hands. She believed it was perfect timing as Christmas items began to trickle in from the children's home. Each year, the items for the auction became more impressive. These were the ones that passed quality assurance.

Ray stopped what he was doing and leaned back in the chair. "How is Landon's grandmother doing? Is her mind current, or is she starting to miss things?"

Gina shrugged. "Honestly, I let Landon lead that discussion. I'm at a crossroads. If I ask about Granny Lonna, I don't know if I'm not adding to his burden to worry about her. On the other hand, if I don't ask about her, I don't want him to think she's not important to me."

"Pray for wisdom, and God will guide the words. Just because someone isn't saying anything doesn't mean they aren't suffering alone," her father advised, then returned to his computer.

Okay, Lord, this a Word from You. She hadn't prayed for wisdom. Nodding, Gina finished unwrapping the pieces, inspecting the child's name, age, and year inscribed on the bottom of each piece before taking photos for Landon to show his grandmother. It was important for the children to get recognition for their talents.

The feel of Christmas in July wouldn't be complete without the decorations, and that would come soon, and then there would be no holding back.

Landon came through the doorway with to-go containers filled with sandwiches and salad. She walked out to the lobby to meet him.

"Hi, Mr. Christmas. Hey, baby." After kissing her cheek, he rested the bags on the counter, which were enough for all three. Landon shook her father's hand, then glanced around at the decor. He sniffed and chuckled. "Is that gingerbread and nutmeg I smell?"

"Scented candles." Her father chuckled. "That's my daughter's ploy to get people to think about Christmas and cooler weather because it's too hot. We add cool treats to the snack box for the Round-Up program. With school starting, students need help with supplies and school uniforms. As I'm sure Gina has told you, families and children are in need every day." His eyes sparkled as he watched Landon embrace her in a hug.

Gina nodded at her father. "What do you think about letting Granny Lonna see these photos?"

Landon was quiet, then kissed her forehead. "That's a good idea. We can go this weekend after the taste testing at the Asian Foundry."

While there, Gina planned to inspect Granny Lonna's items more closely. If those items were from her charity, she would need to see who purchased them. It wouldn't have been a big deal, but because he distrusted charities, she didn't want to give him a reason to think Every Day is Christmas didn't keep accurate records.

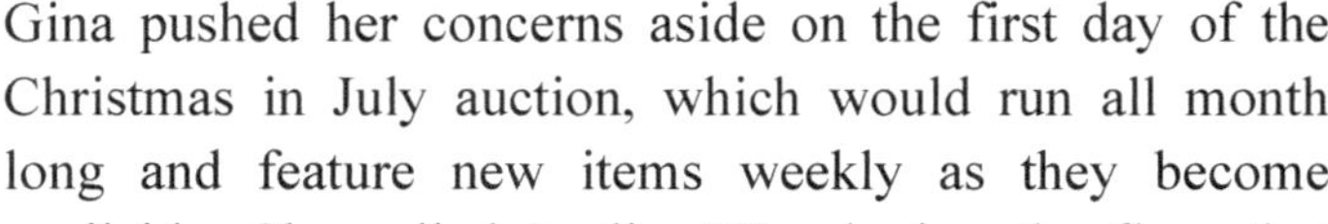

Gina pushed her concerns aside on the first day of the Christmas in July auction, which would run all month long and feature new items weekly as they become available. She called Leslie: "I'm loving the flyer that dropped in my email this morning. Let the bidding begin."

"Yes!" Leslie was charged up. "Melody said the children at the home are working like elves to get their pieces done. As you can see, we're starting with ten and will add more each week. This never gets old." She sighed.

"Not for me either. Talk to you later." Gina called Landon. "Our Every Day is Christmas auction is live!" She giggled, and he chuckled.

"Wow, baby. That's great. Give me the website, and I'll take a look and make sure Granny Lonna looks too."

"Thank you, Landon. It ends the first week in August, and items are shipped immediately. Last year, the children created thirty items. This year, they want to do fifty. But Melody reminded them of quality over quantity. Melody said they quickly lowered the number to forty, which is still more than last year."

Landon didn't interrupt as she rambled while he was on the website, perusing the items. His praise of the pieces made her fall more for him than she already had. When he showed his grandmother the photos on the website, Granny Lonna raved about the artistry but none were what she had in mind.

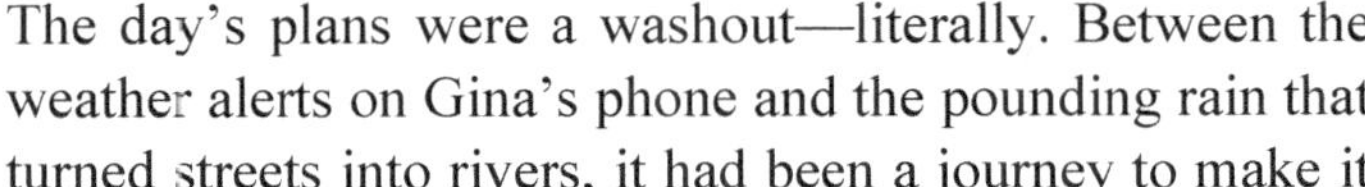

The day's plans were a washout—literally. Between the weather alerts on Gina's phone and the pounding rain that turned streets into rivers, it had been a journey to make it home from her office Friday night, and it hadn't stopped raining all day on Saturday.

"Lord, will it rain forty days and forty nights?" Her voice was barely audible over the relentless rain drumming on her windows and roof. The thunder and lightning didn't ease her worry.

"You will see the rainbow in the sky as My Word says that I will not destroy man by water again," God whispered.

Denise's ringtone interrupted her musing. She was in New York at a sales conference. "Hey. I see St. Louis is making national news with historic flooding. It looks bad. Images of flooding are widespread instead of in one place, usually by the Meramec River. It's close to home. Part of I-70 is underwater, with entire shopping areas and non-stop calls for water rescues. That's scary."

"What?" Gina was glad she told Landon to stay home. While listening to Denise, she padded across her bedroom floor to her home office.

Gina sat at her desk and clicked on the laptop to see what images the world saw about her city.

Her jaw dropped. "Wow." She recognized some of the places at random locations. Some parts of the city had lost power, others had flooding in their basements, and motorists were stranded on parts of the highway due to the rain falling and the sewers unable to keep up.

Another call came through. "Landon's calling me now. I'll keep you posted."

"Okay, sis. Love you. Stay dry."

Landon's deep voice greeted her when she swapped the calls. "You dry over there?"

"I am safe at home." Gina patted her chest. She couldn't imagine getting trapped in flash flood waters. "Where are you? Please tell me you're at home."

"I'm at my house away from you." Landon was quiet. "I miss you. Before I met you, my life was satisfying, but without you, it's empty,"

"*Awww*. I miss you, too." Gina pouted, although she was in a happy place.

Landon huffed. "This is the first weekend I haven't been with you since we've been dating, and I'm not liking it. If I owned a canoe, I'd be at your house now. But I'll use this time to go next door and check on Bradley. Hopefully, the rain will subside by the morning when I come and get you for church."

Gina's eyes were glued to her computer. One breaking news flashed after another. "Uh, babe, some churches are announcing closings because of flooding. A lot of them."

She shivered to shake off the fear. Although she was safe inside her home, others outside were in danger. Gina began to pray for the safety of those impacted wherever they were.

On Sunday, both of their churches were spared flood damage, but en route to her church, the magnitude of the devastation was evident by damaged goods piled at curbs or neighborhoods where cars were in yards instead of parked in the street because of flooding.

Monday morning wasn't business as unusual as Gina maneuvered through flood detours to get to the office downtown.

Some businesses, like Christmas Tax Help for All Seasons, were unaffected, but others suffered moderate water damage or power outages.

Her father had arrived first. He packed up folders to take and secured others to leave in a safe area. "Grab whatever you need and work from home. It's going to be a rough week. The electricity is out across the street."

Gina did as her dad instructed, then headed home a few hours later with files. On the way, she called Landon. "Some families in U-City have lost a lot of stuff, so I gave a sizable donation today. I went to high school with many of the residents there."

Landon was quiet.

"Babe, are you still there?" She stopped at a light.

"I hope the money gets to them. The news is warning people of scams when disasters hit. This is exactly why I don't give money. You can't trust people. We can give by volunteering together at a shelter."

"You do you, Landon, and I'll do me. I give, pray, and have faith the right people will get it. I'd rather do that than volunteer."

Landon huffed, and Gina heard coworkers' voices in the background. "Listen, baby, my comfort zone is doing and seeing that I make a difference."

"And I'm not trying to be selfish, but I need my downtime." Christmas Tax Help for All Seasons was a small two-person business. Her boyfriend witnessed it firsthand when one person was out. "That's not an option for me right now."

"That's why I said it's something we can do together. I have money to give, but it's staying in my bank account, no exceptions."

Gina shook her head. This man was unbelievable. "Landon, this is not Haiti, Katrina, or other world disasters. These are our local neighbors in our backyards. I can't take time away from work to help, and my donations will go farther."

"Baby, haven't you heard a word I said? The news is alerting people of scammers. Unbelievable. I have no problem buying food, blankets, or essential supplies and materials, not money."

"Half the city probably needs it. You're overthinking this."

"No, you're vulnerable. You're setting yourself up to be a victim. The criminals will alert another scammer that they've got a sucker and target you for more money."

Victim? Vulnerable? Target? And sucker? Gina was ticked now. Another call interrupted their conversation before Gina said something she would regret. "Bye, Landon."

"Gina, this is Melody Ransom. Bad news."

"Oh no." Gina's heart seemed to stop, and her breath escaped her. "What happened?" She prayed none of the children were hurt.

"Well, some of the most beautiful ornaments they've ever created were damaged by floodwaters. Thank God no children were downstairs working, but they are devastated."

Gina exhaled as her heart dropped. She could hear Landon saying, *"Money won't fix this."* Although Gina had deadlines to meet with audits, whether she worked at home or in the office, this situation was personal. "I'll be there as soon as I can today."

At home, she couldn't concentrate, so she closed down her computer and headed to the children's home. It was worse than Gina could have imagined. The basement workshop the children used was obliterated. Remnants of angels and other Christmas items were floating in a foot of water that was still being pumped out.

Gina did her best not to cry in front of the children. She sniffed to bear the ache of disappointment in her heart. "Melody, I want you to submit a request for emergency funds, city grants, and donations from supporters." She came out of her pocket with the needed funds for supplies for a makeshift studio in an upper room to keep the students' minds off the disaster.

"Okay." The woman also did her best to show composure, but the worry in her eyes spoke of her hurt.

"FEMA should be in St. Louis today, and hopefully, our governor will declare a State of Emergency. Agencies and local organizations have money. The state and federal government should step in after that with funds."

"Miss Gina!" Jodi, a brilliant seven-year-old, shouted and ran to her.

Melody didn't scold the girl about the etiquette of not interrupting, and Gina was glad. She looked up with tears in her eyes. "We won't have anything to sell now."

Gina huffed. *I know*. The school needed money to buy supplies. For Granny Lonna's sake, Landon was invested too. Too bad they weren't speaking.

Chapter Sixteen

Landon hadn't spoken to Gina in almost a week. He didn't like it, but he didn't like arguing with her either. It felt awkward for him to show up at his church solo. He told himself that she was just a visitor, so why did members seem surprised to see him without her?

He had been busy, and so had she. Landon filled the void with visits to his grandmother.

Stubborn. That's what Granny Lonna called him for not checking on Gina. She was in her element. At any other time, Landon would have been ecstatic, but because of the subject matter, Landon was uncomfortable.

"I've been busy" was not a sufficient answer. "People's houses and livelihoods were destroyed or damaged. I am working, and my company allows employees to volunteer with the cleanup."

It was odd that Gina had asked to visit Granny Lonna before the flooding. Now, his grandmother seemed in her present mind and asked about Gina repeatedly.

Women. Landon sighed. They were ladies whom he loved dearly.

Granny Lonna's graying eyes stared into his. An unreadable expression played on her face. Was she trying to remember something or carefully gathering her words? "I'm eighty-two, you know, and you've yet to live half my age. If you care for that beautiful, sweet woman, compromise, apologize, and see how far your relationship will go. Pray for the words to say. You want the right woman to hold your hand during this walk on earth."

Landon nodded but didn't entirely agree. When it came to money, he liked to follow the trail. What was wrong with that? *Nothing*, he answered himself. Yet, Landon was miserable without seeing Gina. Why did he feel guilty? That emotion he didn't like. She had seeped into his being, and he desperately missed her.

"Okay," Landon said, and they finished eating dinner. Restless, he watched a few game shows on television with her. His mind was elsewhere on how to fix this. A silly idea came to him. If anyone had what he needed, his grandmother did.

"Granny Lonna, do you have any unused Christmas cards?"

Her eyes lit up. "Why, yes. It's May, but you can never start too early to stock up because every year they get more expensive…"

Happiness mixed with sadness. It was July. It was great that she had unused cards, but not so great that his grandmother was two months behind. He exhaled. Her condition was bothering him more.

"It's kind of early to send them out, don't you think?" She squinted, tapping on her thin lips. "It's almost Mother's Day."

Go with the flow, he coaxed himself. Hopefully, her fog would clear up soon. Landon held on to that glimmer of hope as he held up one finger. "All I need is just one." His grandmother always seemed to have whatever he needed growing up; even now, she came through for him.

Granny Lonna stood, and he helped her. With a steady hold on his arm, she led him to her stash and beamed at her stockpile. They rambled through it together until Landon found a card with a picturesque scene of a storefront with a wreath on the door and snow-covered ground surrounding the building. *Let It Snow…*was scribbled outside in a fancy handwriting style.

Inside, it read: *May the Lord's blessing be abundant as snow as we celebrate joy to the world, peace on earth, and the many gifts He brings to us.*

Perfect. Landon already knew the message he would add. "Got it, Granny Lonna," he said, then helped her in bed for a nap. He kissed her cheek.

She looked at him as Landon covered her with her favorite red throw blanket. "I know you love her, so fix it. Good night." She closed her eyes, and her lips curled into a smile.

He left her house, praying, "Lord, please keep her mind stable so she can enjoy the one thing she wants for Christmas, in Jesus' name, Amen."

As Landon drove home, his grandmother's words echoed in his mind. Perhaps Gina's confidence in giving was because she knew how to follow the money trail. He parked in his driveway but didn't get out. His mind was consumed with thoughts.

Without realizing what he was doing, Landon texted her.

I love you and miss you.

Then he waited for a reply. His phone showed his text was delivered but not read. After a few moments longer of waiting and no response, Landon stepped out of his vehicle and walked into his house.

Once inside his kitchen, he took the greeting card out of his inner coat pocket. He reread the words and realized there was so much to say. The card wasn't large enough to hold his emotions. Landon added to the card, *You are my Christmas gift every day. Love you, Landon.*

Landon knew her street and the house, but couldn't remember the address to mail it. He could always hand deliver it, but considering they weren't on speaking terms, he'd rather save himself the embarrassment if she wouldn't answer the door and invite him inside, so he sent it to the company address. "She's not going to call or text me back," he mumbled as he grabbed his keys and returned to his car for a quick drive to the post office's drop box.

An hour later, when he was about to shower and go to bed, his phone chimed with an alert.

I miss you too. Tired. Back hurts. Aching muscles. Helping with cleanup at children's home and getting ready to soak in a tub.

Hmmm. Although he didn't mind using his muscles for cleanup, he would rather she didn't overdo it and hurt herself.

Her response gave Landon hope that all communication hadn't been severed. **Give me the address, and I'll come tomorrow after work to help.**

When Gina did just that, a smile tugged at his lips. "Lord, is there any way Gina and I can compromise on this? I really love her."

"I commanded twelve apostles with twelve personalities, and they performed My will. Pray, and I'll give you wisdom to figure it out," God whispered.

Gina's heartbeat was off, filled with a mix of anticipation and nervousness when Landon walked into the children's home dressed in his worn jeans, long-sleeve T-shirt, and gloves tucked in his back pocket. His eyes seemed to search the room for her, and they connected. Her heart was jumpstarted.

His smile was inviting and conveyed that all was well with them. Neither had apologized for their stubbornness. Gina wanted to abandon her wash bucket to run to him, demand his hugs, get lost in his embrace, and tell him she was sorry for her attitude. Desperation for his attention had crept in.

Would an audience of curious teenagers and unfamiliar adults hold her back?

"I'm here to help." Landon's strong voice gained everyone's attention. His neighbor Bradley was beside him.

Whew. Regulate your breathing, girl, and get back to work, she chided herself.

Melody stood from her squatting position in the corner. "Landon, right?" Relief flooded her face. "We can use your help. Follow me to the next room where the men are cutting and removing the soggy drywall."

Seeing him and hearing his voice made Gina remember how often they spoke throughout the day and his visits to her office to drop off lunch.

Gina had come to encourage the young artists that all hope wasn't gone for them to recover from the loss, and Melody put her to work, salvaging what could be, which was very little. The pieces destroyed had been the most creative she had seen in the five years since she had created the partnership with the children's home.

The headmistress gathered the children for bed while the handful of adults finished what they could do for the night. Many had to work the next day like her. Gina heard heavy footsteps and felt Landon's presence.

"Hey, babe, are you ready to call it a night?" His words were soothing.

Turning around, Gina wrapped her arms around his waist and buried her face into his chest with a sigh. She welcomed the scent of his cologne mixed with sweat from hard labor.

The rhythm of his heartbeat lulled her into a peace of contentment that she didn't want to move from.

"I'm sorry," she heard him say—or maybe it was her, but the words were said. Gina looked up and gazed into his serious but soft eyes before they closed, and he rested his forehead on hers.

Bradley cleared his throat and grinned. "Looks like you two need some privacy to get mushy." He turned and wandered around, but she sensed the teenager was still watching them. Who cared? She was in Landon's arms.

"I still owe you a weekend of pampering once all this is under control."

Smiling, Gina nodded. "I'll eagerly await it."

"Agreed." Landon grabbed two sanitizing wipes, removed her gloves, wiped her hands, and kissed them. "Come on, let me walk you to your car. Bradley and I can trail you home."

Gina balked. "Landon, that's out of your way."

"And I was out of my mind for being petty and saying my opinion was the only way. I won't mentally shut down like that again."

They strolled out of the building with Gina leaning against Landon, not for support but for comfort. Bradley was whistling behind them.

The following day at work, Gina received a red Christmas card. At first, she thought the mail was for a hair salon a few businesses down the block that had asked the Christmases if they could accept their mail until they could get up and running again after the flood.

Gina was surprised it was addressed to her without the sender's information.

She opened the envelope and pulled out a beautiful scenic Christmas card that reminded her of their office after the first snowfall of the year once all the decorations were hung outside.

The words were simple and elegant, but the handwritten line meant the most to her. Landon considered her his gift. Closing her eyes to relish in the moment of bliss, Gina held the card to her chest and sniffled. She called to thank him. It went to voicemail, and seconds later, a text came that he was on a site inspection.

A few days later, flowers arrived at the office, with red and green wired ribbons tied around a summer bouquet.

Gina called to thank him for flowers, but the call went to voicemail. Seconds later, a text came: **I'll call you later. In a meeting. I love you!**

She couldn't wait until their lives were back on track. Unfortunately, romance was not on their side for the next month as they continued to help those who needed it to bounce back from the record summer flood.

Whatever audits Gina didn't finish during the day, she worked on them on the weekends to meet the deadlines.

But the Christmas decorations needed to go up. Gina had to remind people to be generous and not wait until December to be charitable despite many having turned their attention to flood victims needing assistance.

Although Every Day is Christmas had some inventory for the auction, that money was earmarked for the older students' trust fund. She worried about the general items for the Christmas season, as the supply and demand would be off.

Plus, she hadn't forgotten about the items in Granny Lonna's house that possibly came from their store. If she didn't purchase them, then who?

Chapter Seventeen

Gina didn't see him coming. Every Day is Christmas was known for granting at least eighty percent of requests. Leslie Littles made sure of it.

"Gina?" Her father's face came into view.

She jolted. "Sorry, Dad. What were you saying?"

"I said," he stepped aside, and Landon came into view, "Landon is here."

Ray chuckled and walked back into his private office after delivering the letters that came in the mail from Leslie.

"Baby, what's wrong?" Landon sat next to her desk and scooted closer.

Gina was so numb that she didn't answer when she handed him the papers.

He frowned as he read page after page. Landon looked up with a confused expression. "What are these?"

"We have received applications from students in need, and we don't know if our charity can meet them this year. We lost a lot of money on pieces destroyed in the flood."

Her father walked out of his office. "Landon, since you're here, I will leave my daughter in safe hands." Ray kissed her forehead, shook Landon's hand, and walked out the door. She could tell he was just as upset as she was.

Gina withheld her tears until they were alone, prompting Landon to lock the door for a moment of privacy, then he came around her desk. He hugged her. "Baby, talk to me, please."

Her words and her mind were out of sync. After regulating her breathing, she mumbled, "I feel like I have failed my dad and the children."

"Why, baby?" Landon's concerned expression made her want to weep.

Dropping her head, Gina studied her hands. She was ashamed to admit her role in the loss of funds. "I turned away walk-ins. That was lost revenue for our tax business and exposure to information about the silent auction without mentioning it and sales for the Round-Up program."

Landon allowed her to vent without interrupting. If a tear fell, he caught it with his thumb.

"The Round-Up program would have been our charity's backup, but because of the flooding, funding for the arts isn't a priority, which is understandable." Gina took a deep breath and exhaled. "Because of the flooding, very few pieces were salvageable, and I don't think any of the angel ornaments interest your grandmother. With school starting in a few weeks, there's not enough time for the children to make up the inventory."

"Why don't you get your inventory elsewhere to meet the supply?"

"There are a few more high school students, but not as many as those at the children's home, and I feel bad for them. Every Day is Christmas was meant to encourage and spark creativity in young minds and give them hope beyond their circumstances. Some of these children have nothing. The ornaments are part of their signature collection, and they are used to earn money while helping others. It wouldn't be the same. Plus, customers like your grandmother can tell the difference between a budding artist and a seasoned professional. That's what makes our ornament and pieces unique. Customers see the potential before it's manifested—like faith."

"I know faith is for something hoped for and not seen—yet. I'm not seeing that type of vision." Landon shook his head. "And I'm being honest."

Smiling, Gina scooted back so he could see her face entirely. "Look at me and describe me."

He chuckled. "I can close my eyes and see you clearly. Your innocent brown eyes make me guess what you're thinking. Your long lashes and brows seem hand-painted on a portrait. You wear a serious expression while your lips curl in an ever-present faint smile. Your thick, wavy hair is the same shade of brown as your eyes against a complexion that reminds me of pure honey. That wasn't done by accident. God was very precise when He created you."

Choked with emotions, Gina patted her chest. "Wow. I've never heard anyone describe me that way—and with their eyes closed. Are you sure you're seeing me?" she teased.

He pulled out his phone and held up the camera as a mirror for her to see herself. "I notice everything about you, lady."

She leaned forward, and Landon met her halfway for a kiss.

"Sweet," he murmured against her lips.

It was sweet and more.

Gina withdrew first, panting and refocused. "Sorry for venting. Usually, I only subject Denise to my pity parties."

Landon squeezed her hand. "You've got me now. How else will I know what's going on in that beautiful head of yours? Babe, we're in this together. What affects you also touches me. We'll brainstorm. You can bounce ideas off me. I know people, too." He stood and strolled to the nook area, grabbed two water bottles out of the mini fridge, and dropped a ten-dollar bill in the donation box, then unlocked the door for business.

She wanted to cry at his action. Landon was stepping out of his comfort zone. Gina smiled as she accepted the drink. For the first time since his arrival, she admired his collarless mint green short-sleeve shirt, perfect for August weather, with his khakis. He made any color look good. Nothing was ever out of place with him. She was blessed that they had found each other.

"I'm sorry that I'm griping over this when I know your thoughts are on Granny Lonna."

Landon shrugged and twisted the caps off their bottles. "I don't know which is declining more, her health or her mind."

"Yeah. Who knows if one of the children had created the winning Black angel in the batch ruined by water damage? I don't want the children to feel guilty over something beyond their control. The auction ended with twenty-three items." She shrugged and gnawed on her lips. "I wish I could have done more."

"You mean like you're beating yourself up over something beyond your control?" Landon gave her a knowing smile. "Finish up, woman, so we can go. I think you need your man to buy you dinner."

Landon didn't know what contentment was until he met Gina. Life seemed better. The flood disaster allowed them to see the other's side regarding charity. It was an obstacle that they worked through. There was no one way to help.

He also didn't like seeing her stressed about the charity's finances, and he was about to show her how much she had changed him.

The Lord had given them the perfect backdrop for a late summer picnic—high clouds, a gentle breeze, and sunny skies with little humidity. Because of morning commitments, Gina and Landon agreed to meet in Creve Coeur Park, the halfway mark for both of them, where lush green grass cushioned their blanket. The sandwiches, fruit, and cheeses made them sluggish as Gina relaxed her back against his chest.

Landon inhaled the fragrance of her earlier salon visit. He kissed her neck until she giggled with her eyes closed.

"I have a surprise for you."

"What?" She turned around and looked at him, then closed her eyes for a kiss. "What is it?" she mumbled.

"Can't tell you because your sweet lips are distracting me."

That didn't stop her from delivering a few more pecks. "Okay. I'll be good." Gina's eyes brightened with expectancy.

"I want to make a charitable contribution to Every Day is Christmas." He waited for her reaction.

"Huh? You do?" She paused, then spoke slowly. "Thank you, but why?"

Laughing, Landon squeezed her tighter. "One, because I love you. Two, because I don't like to see my beautiful woman stressed out, and three, I'm confident in your ability to manage."

Was that fear or uncertainty in her eyes?

He was about to sweeten the pot. "My family wants to give, too, as do some groups at my church. Everyone loves you and wants to support the worthy cause—children."

Gina looked away and seemed to pick at crumbs falling onto their blanket.

He lifted her chin and pressed his lips against hers, then rested his forehead on hers. "I know this won't replace the items lost due to the flood, but the money will be there when requests like the ones you showed me come in, so your charity won't miss a beat."

"Landon…" Gina's voice was barely above a whisper. Her eyes were misty.

"Yes, babe?" He knew this news would make her happy but he didn't expect the tears. "Thank you for helping me break down my walls of mistrust."

"You're welcome. Will you take me to Granny Lonna's house?"

That was an unexpected subject switch. "Sure, babe." Something wasn't right. Gina's reaction didn't match the good news. "It's Labor Day weekend. My dad plans to barbecue."

Gina seemed to gather her composure as she looked into his eyes. Instead of happiness, sadness stared back at him. "Before I can accept your money, I need to check out some pieces that your grandmother has from our inventory. I've searched records, and I can't find any record of her buying them."

Be careful, stay calm, ask the right questions, and don't jump to conclusions. Landon's breath caught. He counted to three, watching her before he exhaled and mustered a slight chuckle he wasn't feeling. "Explain."

"Well, we know Granny Lonna didn't steal them. The sales and the items balance, so our records are okay, but if she has been buying them yearly, why do I only see one entry for her? I've been working on a discovery for months, and nothing seems off."

"Think before you speak because you won't be able to take it back," God whispered.

"Landon?" Gina said his name twice, but his mouth was glued together.

"Babe, I know if there is a discrepancy, my lovely woman will find it."

Exhaling, Gina wrapped her arms around his waist. "Thank you. Thank you."

Good save, God, because that's not close to what I was about to say.

"Come on. Let's get ready to go there now."

This was a mystery that should have been solved on day one. But Gina would never hear Landon say that—he hoped, at least.

Chapter Eighteen

Unknowingly, Gina was tortured by not going to see Granny Lonna as Landon had said. The reason was that his grandmother had unexpected visitors who overstayed and tired her out. Now, she was resting for a few days.

That was a week ago, and Gina felt he was essentially holding his grandmother hostage.

"Who knew love would be so complicated?" Denise *tsk*ed as the two sisters prepped the meat at their parents' house for the grill.

Gina exhaled and shook her head. She still couldn't believe it. "Talk about bad timing. He told me how I had made a believer out of him to support charities—our charity." Her heart ached to discuss it.

"Well, sis, I don't know what to tell you. You said he came into the relationship with an attitude, and you two seemed to have worked around it, so…" Denise shrugged, giving advice on relationships without being an expert.

Her sister desired a relationship but avoided them for fear of getting hurt. Gina had become the test case. "Only God can change a person's heart."

"Which God did do," Gina snapped, then apologized and huffed. "Those unaccounted for pieces are messing with my head."

Denise was about to hug her, but Gina stepped out of the way. "Don't you dare until you wash your hands."

The sisters laughed, and then Gina sobered. "I know it's not mismanagement, but it's bugging me."

"What mismanagement?" their father's voice boomed from the doorway.

The sisters exchanged glances before Gina answered. "There's no mismanagement, Daddy..." She felt like a little girl again. "It's about the Black angel ornaments Landon's grandmother has."

Ray walked into the kitchen, carrying a blue oven pan filled with barbecued meat. "What does that have to do with mismanagement?" Resting it on the counter, he waited for an explanation. Whenever he wore his small, black-framed glasses, he looked intimidating.

"It's not," Gina quickly answered. "We were talking about Landon's grandmother's cute little bungalow in a retirement community. Her front rooms look like a scene from Santa's showroom, with amazing Christmas decorations and knickknacks. I recognized three pieces from the children's home inventory."

Her father frowned at her rambling.

"Our records only show she purchased one piece, so why does she have three?"

"Maybe they didn't come from Every Day is Christmas charity. It could have been a gift," her mother, who had begun to peel potatoes, offered as an explanation.

"True." Gina nodded and washed her hands. The perk of being on the board of directors is seeing the items before they go to the charity to be cataloged and auctioned. I'm familiar with our collection."

"How long have you been overthinking this?" Ray asked.

Denise twirled around and lifted a finger in the air as if she was leaving the sanctuary.

Traitor, Gina thought.

"Don't go anywhere," their father ordered. "This is a family business, which means anything associated with the Christmases must be above suspicion. Most bookkeeping irregularities are simply mistakes until proven otherwise. This isn't a forensic mission. Have you asked Landon to clear up the confusion?"

"Landon didn't know I was trying to figure it out on my own and obsessing over it."

"You are such a worry wart." Their mother wrapped her arm around Gina's shoulder. "I'm reminded of lyrics from 'What a Friend We Have in Jesus. O what peace we often forfeit, o what needless pain we bear, all because we do not carry everything to God in prayer!' Landon should have been the first person you asked, then you would have been able to sleep at night."

"Landon was already suspicious—"

"Probably still is," Denise mumbled.

"You aren't helping. He intimidated me. That would have hinted at improprieties."

"Well, where is he now?"

Gina sat on the stool. "We haven't spoken in a few days since I mentioned it to him. I've been waiting for the 'I'll call you.'" She did air quotes.

"I'm praying there is a simple explanation that was overlooked," her mother said. "I miss seeing you and Landon together at church. I was hoping Landon would be our first son-in-law."

"Denise might have to deliver that gift to you."

"Me?" Her sister patted her chest. "I'm not dating."

"Well, you may be our only hope." Gina walked away to the powder room to wipe away her tears.

"You made this a big deal," the devil taunted her.

"I'm her problem solver. Come to me," God overrode the accusation.

It was an emotional setup. Landon had poured out his soul to the woman he loved, and Gina had a concern that involved him—or his grandmother—and she hid it from him.

Landon had been bummed out since that day and was glad when Terrell called to say he was in town and wanted to get together and meet Gina. He couldn't make good on the last part, so the best friends met at a sports bar as Landon tried to analyze his feelings.

"Man, I almost seriously gave up some money because of her."

Terrell chewed on his steak and fries, then looked at him. "Bro, my question is, was she trying to deceive you or not? People make mistakes."

"Not with my money." He pushed away his empty plate and leaned back in his chair. "An accountant's job is to balance books." Landon rubbed his forehead. "I love her."

"Love keeps no record of wrongs," God whispered First Corinthians thirteen. *Read My Word.*

"Then work it out with her, man." Terrell raised his hand for the check. When the server arrived, Landon swiped it.

"My treat, T. You're cheaper than a trained counselor." Landon reached for his wallet.

Terrell laughed. "That would be the wrong profession for me."

Landon nodded. When deciding their majors in college, they both encouraged the other to go for the money and choose fields where minorities were underrepresented and paid well. Law and engineering were the answer. That's when the idea of becoming role models surfaced.

"Bro, everything will work out," Terrell said as he stood and left a twenty-dollar bill as a tip.

Landon looked around and spied their server at another table. He picked up the tip and took it to her.

She smiled her thanks.

Terrell chuckled as they stepped outside. His friend slipped on his pricey sunglasses, and they began their stroll to their cars. Of course, Terrell's rental was a luxury model. "You really do have trust issues, and yet Gina fell in love with you anyway."

Landon said nothing.

"Man, you're the one who scared her off. Poor Gina," he said, Landon believed to irritate him. "She trusted you, and you left her hanging." Terrell paused. "You've got one day to make it right before I leave town so I can meet Gina Christmas. After that, I'm not sure when I'll be back this way with court cases and conferences."

The two friends shook hands, patted each other on the back, and went their separate ways.

By the time Terrell flew back to Washington, D.C., Landon hadn't met his one-day deadline.

Chapter Nineteen

The day marked another Sunday when Landon showed up at his church without Gina.

Landon's solution was to skip the in-person service and visit with Granny Lonna.

"There's my favorite grandson," she said with open arms when he walked through the door. "You're early, aren't you?"

Hugging her, Landon sniffed the scent of his grandmother's life-long favorite body lotion. "Yep. We can watch the service online together." He trailed her to her kitchen, since her living and dining rooms seemed pre-staged for Christmas elves. Pointing the remote to her television monitor on the wall near the table, Landon clicked on the social media platform that would air the church service.

She squinted up at Landon when she sat. "Where's Gina, my Black angel?"

If Landon didn't answer, she would keep asking. He stalled, scrambling for what to say. "Can I get you anything while I'm here?"

"Yes, an answer." She frowned.

"Granny Lonna…" He gritted his teeth. First Terrell, now his grandmother. "I haven't spoken to her in a couple of days." Almost a week. Was Gina counting, too?

"I thought you loved that girl. Well…" she rocked back in her chair, which wasn't a rocker and patted her legs, "…as sweet as she is, some good man is going to love her the way she deserves to be loved." Folding her arms, Granny Lonna stiffened like a defiant child and grunted. "Thought that was my grandson. All a woman wants is a man who will love her when she's happy or sad. It's an everyday love, not once in a while or when a man's not mad at her. A wife is a gift from God. You know Adam had everything at his fingertips, but God gave him a wife for companionship."

Soft gospel music announced the live stream service had started. His grandmother didn't stop talking as Landon guided her into the family room to her recliner. He didn't need a sermon now. His grandmother had already preached one. "Granny Lonna, what are you saying?"

Suddenly, she was quiet.

Landon squinted to make sure she hadn't suddenly fallen asleep as he sat beside her and stretched his legs.

"*Shhh.* Pastor's singing my favorite song." Closing her eyes, Granny Lonna hummed the lyrics, "Nobody Like the Lord."

Her voice was weak, but the harmony could still soothe Landon's downcast spirit. "It's almost Christmas, grandson. Get your grandmother a beautiful ornament this year, and don't come back without Gina," Granny Lonna said fifteen minutes into the sermon.

Did that mean any ornament would do? "Okay." Landon had expected her to say the Black angel ornament. Since she didn't, he could order online at any specialty store and end the hunt.

Granny Lonna's other request might be more challenging.

He stood and kissed her, then said his goodbye.

In his vehicle, Landon gave himself a pep talk. It didn't seem like he could keep Gina away from Granny Lonna, even if he wanted. Taking a chance, he drove across town to Christ Has Risen, Gina's church, hoping to get there before the service dismissed.

A couple of ushers recognized him and were about to sit Landon in the sanctuary with Gina, but he asked for a back row in a different section to see if Gina was there.

Spotted. She sat with her family.

"Saints, as I conclude my sermon today," Pastor Swelling said, closing his Bible, "meditate this week on the fruits of the Spirit as in Galatians five, verses twenty-two to twenty-three. Were you paying attention this morning?"

"Yes," members surrounding Landon said.

"Remember those fruits that God planted in you when the Lord filled you with the Holy Ghost: love, joy, peace, forbearance, kindness, goodness, faithfulness, gentleness, and self-control…

"If you yield to the Holy Ghost, you will bear these fruits. If you're struggling to blossom, come to the altar and let the ministers pray for you so that you will grow abundantly to reflect Christ in your life."

Landon stood. His heart pounded with nervousness as he walked to the altar, where familiar faces greeted him with sincere smiles.

"Praise the Lord, Brother Landon," Minister Cole greeted him. "What can I pray for you today?"

"The fruits—" As he spoke, Landon felt Gina's presence beside him before she slipped her fingers through his.

"Pray for us," Gina told the minister and squeezed Landon's hand.

Peace. Landon felt that fruit immediately. He surrendered as the Holy Ghost's power engulfed his being. Releasing the sins that had tormented him for days, Landon repented and worshipped God. When he opened his eyes, Gina was wiping tears from her eyes, too.

"Love covers a multitude of sins," God whispered. *"Read First Peter four."*

To some onlookers, they could only speculate why Landon and Gina were at the altar. Maybe they thought he and Gina had yielded to fornication, but their sin—or rather his sin—was a heart issue that prohibited him from showing the fruits of gentleness with Gina—patience, understanding, and so much more that wasn't like God.

While several requested the baptism in Jesus' name, Landon followed Gina back to her seat, where the Christmases welcomed him warmly. Sitting there with her, hands linked, Landon felt contentment again.

Counting down to the offering and dismissal, Landon turned to Gina. "Can I steal you?"

"Yes." Her smile lit her beautiful face.

If she forgave him, he wouldn't leave her side again. "Thank you, and I'm sorry for shutting you out. Let me follow you home so you can leave your car. My grandmother misses you, but not as much as me."

The relief on her face saddened Landon, knowing he had hurt her. He would make it right.

<hr>

Once Landon took her home, Gina cried hard in his arms as he smothered her with kisses mixed with their whispered apologies.

Once they confirmed that everything was good between them, they left for Granny Lonna's house.

"You're quiet over there." Landon's baritone voice was comforting as they held hands as he drove them to Granny Lonna's house.

Gina smiled. Her eyes were closed as she thrived in the moment. "Enjoying my happy place with you."

"Amen."

Soon, they arrived at the retirement community. Landon *humph*ed when he parked his SUV. "My family is here. I hope everything is okay. It was earlier." He jumped out of the vehicle and hurried around to get her.

At the front door, Landon fumbled with his key until Mr. Michaels opened it.

Gina looked at his father. She held her breath and began to pray. Had something happened to Granny Lonna?

"Dad, why are you here?" Panic was in his voice as he forced his way into the house. "Is everything okay?"

His father smiled at Gina. "It's good to see you."

What was going on? Gina wanted to know, too.

"Is that my Landon?" Granny Lonna's voice called from the kitchen.

Gina and Landon hurried back.

"Oh, you brought my beautiful Black angel." She opened her arms for Gina, and Gina hugged Landon's grandmother, relieved she was okay.

Landon paced the kitchen floor. "Okay, somebody tell me what is going on."

Janay raced through the door at full speed until she saw her grandmother and collapsed in her father's arms.

"Granny Lonna wanted a lot of company today," Landon's mom began, "because she told us to come over because she had a feeling Landon would make up with Gina."

"How did she know that?" Gina asked. Only God knew what was going to happen today.

"She was right." Landon pulled Gina close for a hug. "I guess she was sure you would forgive me."

"That's worth celebrating." Granny Lonna *shh*ed everyone, so Gina would sit next to her. "I've missed you. What have you been up to?"

Gina thought Granny Lonna reminded her of her grandma Lydia when Gina was a child.

Landon exhaled and murmured she was about to give them a heart attack.

After listening to the women's chatter about Christmas, Landon returned to the kitchen. "Granny Lonna, do you mind showing Gina your collection?"

His grandmother beamed as he helped her to her feet. She started in the dining room while his mother and sister warmed up the meatloaf, mashed potatoes, and mixed vegetables left over from the day before.

Landon remained at his grandmother's and Gina's side. Granny Lonna's memory was top-notch when she talked about the expanded train set, nutcrackers, and several nativity sets—in crystal, gold, and multi-colored—next to the angels, which seemed to be her favorite pieces.

"What about the ornaments, Granny Lonna?" Landon asked, guiding her across the hall to the living room, where there was no shortage of ornaments to decorate the tree.

Gina's nerves were on high alert as she approached the mantel where an angel tree topper stood at attention.

A young girl named Pearl created it about three years ago. The piece showcased her talent, and she was awarded a full college scholarship to the Art Institute of Chicago. Gina delicately picked up the item and looked at the bottom to confirm Pearl's name, along with the year it was created.

"Granny Lonna, was this the first piece you won at auction from our Christmas shop?"

The elderly woman frowned. "Oh no, dear. That was a gift from an old friend, Zettie Mays. Zettie got me hooked on that Christmas store and those children's creations. I love it."

The passion was touching. Gina nodded as she exhaled. That explained that piece.

"This ornament," Granny Lonna said, touching a mini globe-shaped ornament anchored on a stand. It showcased a Black angel with butterfly wings painted purple, red, and gold. "I bought this one myself last year."

Umm-hmm. Our records showed that.

"It's stunning," Landon said in awe. "I see why you believe in these children. They have incredible talent."

"Yes, I know." Gina felt Godly proud that she had created a platform for these children to thrive and earn money. For many of them, this talent was a ticket out of poverty.

Gina listened patiently as Granny Lonna discussed several pieces until she got to the last one, which made Gina curious.

"This Black angel is a ballerina in flight." Granny Lonna smiled. The design wasn't elaborate, but the texture was smooth, shaved wood. The detail in the body and wings was impressive. This looked like one of the first pieces created when she started the charity. Gina carefully angled the figurine to read the bottom. Blank. Not theirs. She frowned.

Granny Lonna told them, "I found it at an estate sale years ago for ten dollars. A bargain."

It was possible that it was theirs. The first year, she and Denise put stickers on the items, so the stickers may have rubbed off.

"Well, I'm tired now," Granny Lonna said, sounding winded. "That's enough for today. Let's eat."

Gina kissed her cheek and smiled at Landon, then mouthed, "All is well."

Chapter Twenty

Landon stepped back when he opened the door to Christmas Tax Help for All Seasons. "Whoa." He was not expecting to see a transformation. It was like a visit to his grandmother's house.

A stockpile of decorations was dumped on Gina's desk. When she peeked up, Landon let out a hearty laugh. It was only mid-October, and already, Christmas had come to town. "Tax services by day, Christmas store by night…in a sense."

"It's a family tradition like Ted Drewes Frozen Custard in the summer and a Christmas tree lot in the winter." Gina smiled.

"You've got a point. They have the best frozen custard." Landon nodded and craned his neck for her father.

Mr. Christmas stuck his head out of his office, walked out, and greeted Landon with a handshake. "I wouldn't laugh too hard, young man. This could be your house one day."

"Never," Landon teased and chuckled.

"You have no idea what you got yourself into, Landon, being around us during the holidays." Her father nodded.

"Yes, I do." He glanced at Gina. "I've got 'Joy to the World,' 'It's the Most Wonderful Time of the Year,' and 'All I Want for Christmas is You' all wrapped in a present with the prettiest bow."

Gina blushed, and Landon slid an arm around her waist and kissed her curls.

He loved her; she knew that, and everyone in their families knew that. It was the quest Granny Lonna sent him on, making him suspect she knew it, too. After the altar prayer and spending time with his grandmother, he and Gina were committed to each other and wouldn't let any other misunderstandings keep them apart.

Plus, Gina and Granny Lonna were a perfect match because they loved Christmas. Whenever Landon brought Gina to visit, he became invisible to the two. Landon wouldn't have it any other way. His grandmother came to life around Gina.

Yep, he knew exactly what he was getting into. "I have no regrets. I've been in the Christmas spirit since meeting your beautiful daughter."

"Good answer." Mr. Christmas turned and walked back into his office.

"So, babe, what's all this?"

"It's time to start decorating for Christmas." Her warm smile wowed him.

"It's kind of early, isn't it?" Landon thought about it. "Halloween is still weeks away, but I'd rather see

Christmas decorations instead of one giving Satan and all his demons a national day of celebration."

Gina abandoned the tangled mess on her desk and reached for her handbag.

Landon was treating her to lunch before the weather turned chilly. It was already sweater weather, and Gina was sporting a thick gold one with flirty but always professional sleeves.

He helped her slip her arms into an off-white blazer, bid goodbye to her father, and walked out the door, hand-in-hand, down Washington Avenue to the Thai restaurant two blocks away.

Once they were seated at their table, Landon continued to hold her hand, briefly thinking about their first date here and how they responded to the homeless man. Besides the day he surrendered to Jesus, that had been the second-best day. He grinned. "Since I've been at my place, I stick a wreath on the door, get some scented candles, and I'm done."

"Ha. That is about to change. You're just getting started." Gina leaned forward and met him halfway for a brief kiss. "My family's tradition is decorating each other's houses. And we're coming for you."

Landon laughed. "Come on, baby."

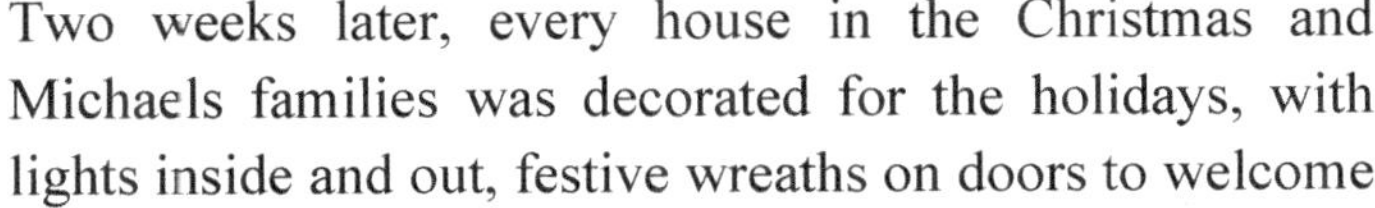

Two weeks later, every house in the Christmas and Michaels families was decorated for the holidays, with lights inside and out, festive wreaths on doors to welcome guests, and nativity ensembles. It had been accomplished as weekend projects, and even Bradley came over to Landon's to help and be nosey.

"Aren't we a big, happy family?" Denise teased more than once as they assisted in preparing snacks in Granny Lonna's kitchen, their last stop.

Gina beamed and jutted her chin. "It's our favorite time of the year, sis."

"Umm-hmm." Denise grinned. "Look at our parents and Landon's. I'm feeling in-law vibes."

"They get along, and Granny Lonna is soaking up the attention."

Denise rested the teakettle and bit her bottom lip, masterminding a scheme, "I've seen Landon and Dad huddled together untangling the lights. Maybe they're having a special conversation." Denise was seriously plotting her future again. "He'll probably propose at Thanksgiving dinner, and you two will have a beautiful, snowy Christmas wedding."

"Wow." Gina gave her sister a dumbfounded expression. "And all that in six weeks." Shaking her head, Gina dismissed Denise's musings. Her single status was in Landon's hands. They'd worked out their differences, and she knew that Landon loved her. As if to prove it, Landon and his family had made a sizable donation to her charity. She was speechless when Leslie at the foundation told her the good news. She had cried in his arms. He was willing to compromise, and she had to learn to do the same.

Black angel ornaments had been mentioned more than a future together.

Hours later, after all the fun had been had, everyone called it a night.

"What church are you two visiting tomorrow?" Landon's mom asked.

She and Landon looked at each other and shrugged. They had grown comfortable at both churches and no longer kept score on whose turn to visit on Sundays.

"Babe, I'm feeling Christ Has Risen Church," Landon said. "I'd have no problem changing memberships."

She felt the same way about his church. Although Pastor Swelling preached a shorter message, Gina liked it when he stopped service if one soul was ready to repent on the spot and be baptized with water and spirit in Jesus' name.

This was an exciting time for her and Landon. Gina couldn't wait to see what was coming next.

Chapter Twenty-one

*D*ate night.

Instead of going out for a night on the town, Landon suggested keeping it low-key because he'd had a rough week on the site of a historic building that caught fire. The remaining structure needed to be demolished, but there was asbestos. Because of public safety, multiple agencies had to work together to get the job done.

Landon wasn't a complainer, but Gina could tell he was irritated with the red tape and disappointed he was too busy to see her throughout the week for lunch.

A low-key date night would be a home-cooked meal and a surprise.

When the bell rang, Gina checked her makeup and smiled. She opened the door, and her jaw dropped with one look at her honey. "Wow."

Against the backdrop of a chilly November evening, Landon stood with a black fedora and a dark wool coat. He lifted his hat in greeting and crossed the threshold into her house. "My lady," he said in a terrible British accent, handing her flowers from behind his back.

"You look too handsome to stay in instead of going out to show you off." Resting her hands on his chest in her sock-covered feet, she stood on her toes to greet him.

"So do you." Landon shook off his coat and hung it on a wall hook. Rubbing his hands, he sniffed. "Something smells good. Need help with anything?"

"Nope. I left work early to prepare mostaccioli. Garlic bread is in the oven, then…" She paused and grinned, "I want to show you my Christmas calendar."

He grabbed her around her waist and gave her a curious expression. "Is this another one of your family traditions?"

"Nope. Just something I created a few years ago, and Denise, not wanting to be a team player, didn't want to play along." She sniffed her bouquet and led the way to the kitchen.

"I'm a team player. I see the salad fixings…and an indoor grill. What are we doing?" He proceeded to wash his hands in the sink.

"That's for the lettuce."

He turned around, leaned against the sink, and folded his arms. "Huh? Ah, babe, that's for meat, vegetables, and bread."

She pulled him to the counter, then bumped him with her hip. "Lettuce is a vegetable, but we're going to make a couple of Caesar salad bites."

Landon chuckled. "So, is this what a man can look forward to when he comes home from work?"

Was this a hint of what would come? Maybe her sister knew about Landon's intentions. Clearing her thoughts, she began to show him a twist on Caesar salad.

"Take four whole hearts of romaine and place them on the grill for thirty seconds."

Landon snickered and shook his head. "Learn something new every day."

"I found the recipe in *Southern Living* magazine online. The article said the grilling would give it a sweet flavor, and they were right. I made this a few times when Denise and I experimented on dishes. Okay, separate the leaves and place them in the platter." She coached him.

"I'm a chef!" Landon exclaimed.

Gina laughed. "Yes, you are, baby." She kissed his cheek and turned away, but he guided her back and kissed her lips.

Briefly, Gina wondered if this was how it felt to be married—contentment doing the simplest tasks. She dismissed her musing and returned to the present. "Take them off, then spoon the dressing on it to your liking. Add chopped cucumbers, diced tomatoes, chopped parsley, and croutons." She waited as he followed her instructions as an alarm sounded. "Oh, that's my timer. The garlic bread is done, so let's eat."

Landon blessed their food, and they ate. They were stuffed after Gina served a slice of store-bought red velvet cheesecake for dessert.

"Great food, gorgeous company, and more," Landon said as they restored her kitchen.

He dried his hands and guided her to the living room, where Gina had flames blazing in the gas fireplace. "So school me, woman, on *our* tradition."

"I like the sound of that." Gina hurried to her desk. She grabbed a twelve-month wall calendar and scooted next to him.

"What's this?"

"Well, we met in March. In April, we spent time together at the office but weren't dating."

Landon was speechless as he flipped through the months and recognized the dates they had enjoyed. He hugged her as he stuttered to say something. "You are incredible to create these memories. I love you."

Closing her eyes, Gina allowed his words to seep into her heart. They were like medicine for her soul.

"But what's this for November and December?"

She opened her eyes and rested her head on his shoulder. "These are all the events we can attend during the holiday season."

"This is ambitious." Landon looked intimidated.

"I know, but I was hoping you and I could pick and choose."

Landon's face flushed with relief. Of the eight events listed, they agreed on the holiday market and a rap concert. "It's getting late, and it's been a rough week, but I want to ask you something."

"Okay." Gina watched his expression. He seemed serious.

He took her hands in his.

Gina's heart pounded wildly as she coaxed herself to breathe normally. She nodded.

"We have to decide how we will spend Thanksgiving and Christmas."

That didn't sound like a proposal was coming. Why did she allow Denise to put that notion in her head?

Landon was romantic. He wouldn't have her cook and then propose, would he?

"Thanksgiving is my family's favorite holiday." He frowned. "Do you mind spending that day with the Michaels family?"

"Of course not, as long as we can spend Christmas with the Christmases." She smiled as Landon took the pen from her fingertips and scribbled in the date: *Special holiday with my lady.*

Minutes later, he kissed her goodbye and was gone.

"Well," Gina exhaled, leaning on the door, "it wasn't a proposal, but a promise…maybe."

Thanksgiving would be different, and Landon was excited. The extra dinner plate wasn't for Terrell or his neighbor Bradley this year. This was for Gina.

Landon had never experienced so much festiveness in his life. Gina thought it would be cute for them to dress in holiday colors, so he was donning his rust-colored pants and a gold ribbed turtleneck. She would have her shapely figure in the same colors.

Gina was a fan of Landon's winter hat collection: knit caps, fedoras on Sundays, or newsboy caps. Her eyes sparkled when he saw her.

Love. His heart was full. Landon liked to think of her when they were apart, but he'd better hurry to pick her up so they could be on time for Thanksgiving Day service.

When he arrived at her house, her greeting didn't disappoint him, and he smothered her with affection before they ended their kiss.

He sniffed. Landon was like a bloodhound when it came to the fragrance of sweet potato pies. He walked inside, removed his cap, and shook off his jacket. "Babe, are you dropping pies off at your mom and dad's?" He felt guilty that he was the cause of her breaking her family tradition for this holiday, but he would experience the same with his family for Christmas. She hurried to the kitchen, and he followed.

"Nope. This pie is for your family. I'll take the other one to Mom's house tomorrow."

"Honey, my mother and sister are cooking more than enough. You didn't have to bring anything."

Gina teasingly scrunched her nose at him. "You never show up to a party or dinner without a gift."

London held up his hands in surrender. "Yes, Miss Christmas."

"Let me wrap this up." Gina placed the pie in a container, "then I'll get my cape, and we'll be ready to go."

Despite the absence of a ring, something about dressing alike shouted they belonged to each other. And it didn't go unnoticed when they arrived at Kingdom Come Church.

Landon's pastor never held members long for Thanksgiving service. Pastor Kilroy joked he could smell homemade dishes all the way to the church.

Once they settled in their pew, the couple prayed and stood to worship with the choir. The saints celebrated the holiday with praises of joy and thanksgiving until the pastor stepped to the pulpit.

"It is a good day to rejoice. We are alive with a purpose from God to keep living. Otherwise, our time would have transpired, so let's praise the Lord for His kindness, mercy, grace, favor…"

Pastor Kilroy's list was endless. He poured out reasons until he was out of breath. By then, every member was praising God.

"It's no wonder that the Scripture for the sermon is taken from one of the Psalms. In Psalm one hundred and verse four, the Bible says, *'Enter His gates with Thanksgiving and His courts with praise. Give thanks to Him and praise His name.'*" Pastor Kilroy closed his Bible. "There you have it, saints. There is nothing more I can add. Be thankful today, regardless of what you eat and who you eat it with. Don't let a toxic environment on this holiday steal your peace because we know the devil's assignment is to steal, kill, and destroy. Take the peace that God gave us and enjoy your day."

The minister received a standing ovation, blessed the congregation with the benediction, and sent them home.

Landon shook hands with members while others greeted Gina warmly.

"Are you following us back to the house?" his dad asked.

"Yep." Landon linked his fingers through Gina's and trailed others out of the sanctuary.

Once at his grandmother's house, he and Gina were forced to split up. "You have Gina to yourself all the time. This is our time," Granny Lonna fussed, dismissing Landon as if he was no longer her favorite—albeit her only—grandson. Rhonda Michaels guided his lady to the kitchen with her hand on Gina's shoulder, probably to reveal all his secrets.

There were no more secrets except one. Landon grinned as he watched them disappear.

"Have a seat, son." His father chuckled as he kicked off his shoes and flopped on the sofa. "They will give her back."

"I'm not worried." Landon stretched out on the recliner at the end of the sofa. "There's just something about Gina that clicks with me. After our initial misunderstanding…" Landon grunted. "We try to understand each other's differences."

His father nodded. "That's good. So you love her?" His father pointed the remote to the flat screen and scrolled to see which football game would entertain them.

Understatement. "More than I thought I had in me."

He hit pause on the programming. "Does she know?"

"Yep, and I remind her often."

Nothing else was said as they focused on the game.

When dinner was announced, Landon stood to rescue Gina, but she stepped out of the kitchen with a glow.

Landon exhaled. She had survived his mother, sister, and grandmother's prying questions. He hugged her as if they had been separated for days instead of an hour. "I missed you," he whispered for her ears only.

"Me, too."

At the dinner table, his dad said the blessing and thanked God for their food. "And thank you for allowing my son to find happiness."

"Amen," his family echoed as Landon reached for Gina's hand.

Granny Lonna smiled. "I knew you would see what I see, a beautiful Black angel."

Gina stood from the other end of the table to hug his grandmother.

The bliss on his grandmother's face from the embrace would be etched in his mind forever. They hadn't seen another unique ornament or piece they thought she would like, but his grandmother seemed satisfied to call Gina her Black angel.

It was time to move forward in their relationship.

Chapter Twenty-two

Since Thanksgiving, whenever the couple went out on the weekends, it became the norm to dress in matching colors. For Landon, life with Gina was like celebrating the Twelve Days of Christmas in six weeks.

It wasn't uncommon for Landon to receive a couple of invites for Christmas and holiday parties each year, and sometimes, he skipped his own company's Christmas party. Not this year. He wanted to show off his lady's beauty and brains. Landon seized every opportunity to do that at youth mentorship programs, church activities, or other events.

Landon's firm hosted a holiday bonanza in the Ritz-Carlton's ballroom. There was no corner of the room that was left untouched with decorations. A line formed to snap photos in front of a red curtain backdrop with gold stars that seemed to spill from the top. Impressive.

"Wow." Gina sucked in her breath as she scanned the room as he removed her wrap. "Look at those centerpieces made out of candy canes."

"Interesting." Miniature red and green gift boxes created a tower for candy canes.

His boss and coworkers were surprised that he showed up with a stunning plus-one. Gina sizzled in a short gold party dress with tall heels that exposed her polished red toes and brought her closer to his lips.

He matched her in a yellow suede jacket and black slacks. Gina's eyes had sparkled when she'd opened the door. She had allowed him to pick out her dress when they shopped for this event. She'd blushed at the length, shorter than usual to show off her gorgeous legs but modest where she wouldn't feel out of her comfort zone. Landon wouldn't have it any other way.

In turn, she had picked his attire. They entered the ballroom to whispers of "stunning couple," "so that's Landon's girlfriend," and other accolades.

"Landon Michaels, I've never seen you look so distinguished. Who is this beautiful woman?" Ralph, a fellow engineer, was already inebriated.

He turned and whispered to Gina, "Babe, I know you're proud of your last name, but it's up to you if you want me to introduce you by your full name. These folks are going to be drinking, and I'll get upset if someone wants to mock you."

Gina nodded. "Sometimes, it's my open door to testify that Jesus is the reason for the season."

"Okay. This is Gina Christmas, and don't start with the jokes."

Ralph didn't seem too happy to be denied a bit of fun, so he slightly bowed to Gina, then lifted his champagne glass. "Merry Christmas to all!" He turned and walked away.

Landon mumbled and guided Gina to meet others on his team, clients, and friends. Next, they hit the buffet table, piled their plates with holiday favorites, and joined others at a table.

With little effort, Gina wowed them when she disclosed her surname and shared the responsibility that came with it. Landon was in awe of her confidence, beauty, and charm. She even gathered potential new clients for the upcoming tax season.

When they were almost alone at the table, Landon turned to Gina. He scooted his chair closer and took her hands in his. "Thank you for coming. I usually skip these parties because I don't want to come solo. Janay came a few times when she was in town, and when word got out that she was my sister, I had to threaten them to back off."

"Your sister is beautiful."

"Maybe." Landon nodded. "But it's hard to compete against your beauty." He sealed it with a quick, soft kiss.

"I can't get enough of holiday parties—family and friends, but Denise never wants to go with me. She says the accountant association parties are boring."

"I disagree." Landon shook his head. "One is incredibly enchanting."

Gina's heart soared. "She has to attend the radio station's Christmas party because all her clients look forward to going for their recognition and stuff."

Landon massaged her hands. "Now, we have each other, so neither of us has to go alone." He looked into her brown eyes and saw all her love for him. His heart captured the emotion for safekeeping.

The night couldn't get any better when they shared a sweet, good-night kiss at her door.

The following week, Landon didn't complain as he dressed to attend an ethnic Christmas festival with Gina, an event that wasn't originally on Gina's exhaustive holiday activities calendar. It was labeled as a vibrant celebration of diverse holiday traditions from around the globe.

. When he arrived at her house, Landon was surprised that she had put up more Christmas decorations inside than before. He shook his head. "You are Miss Christmas, aren't you?"

"Yep." She grabbed her coat, and they were out the door within minutes.

The two visited more than a dozen vendors and purchased items to add themes to Gina's Christmas collection around the world. They tasted authentic dishes from food trucks and took pictures in photo booths with different countries in the background.

Landon made sure Gina was bundled up as the temperature dropped until it got too chilly for him. After a few hours, it was time for him to call it a night because they planned a big date for the next day.

A big date.

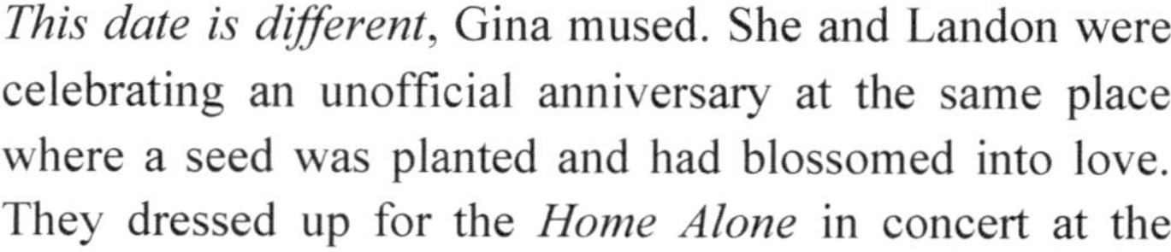

This date is different, Gina mused. She and Landon were celebrating an unofficial anniversary at the same place where a seed was planted and had blossomed into love. They dressed up for the *Home Alone* in concert at the

Stiffel Theatre, where their lives had changed almost nine months earlier.

When she saw this event listed online, she added it to her calendar and circled it more than once. If they didn't go to any other event, this was a "must-attend."

It seemed like Gina had been in a fairytale. She loved romance novels and had learned some movie tropes, and she was living it now with Landon. Their first outing had to be at least two or three tropes with opposites attract, close proximity, and grumpy versus sunshine.

She and Landon had been practically strangers when they attended *Shen Yun*. Tonight, they were a very much in-love couple. It was explosive, and her feelings deepened with one look into his eyes and every touch with his hands.

"Not only do you look beautiful," Landon said, his emotions playing on his face, "but you look so happy." He patted his chest. "And so am I. Did I tell you I love you today?"

"You did." She closed her eyes to inhale the fragrance of love before Gina opened them. "But you can tell me again."

He whispered, and his breath tickled her eyes. Denise, who thought she had become a relationship expert, had been wrong about Landon's Thanksgiving proposal. Gina didn't know why she gave her sister any attention.

Landon's continued profession of love gave Gina hope.

Denise continued to be Gina's cheerleader. Both sisters prayed that December would be the month of an engagement. With thirty-one days in the month, seven were already gone, and still no proposal after any of the events they had attended.

Spending so much time with Landon was a temptation. Lust was real. Gina petitioned the Lord Jesus for help with her growing attraction.

She increased her daily Bible reading, encouraging her to be faithful to holiness.

I can keep you from yielding to temptation, God reminded her every morning in a whisper.

She recited Jude 1:24 throughout the day and nightly after talking with Landon: *Now unto him that is able to keep you from falling, and to present you faultless before the presence of his glory with exceeding joy...*

It was the power of the Holy Ghost that kept them faithful. She exhaled.

Her musing dissipated as the lights faded. The orchestra's instruments set the mood for a relaxing evening. Gina closed her eyes to pray that Jesus delivered her from Landon Michaels's temptation. She craved a marriage proposal like a desperate unemployed person who needed a job offer.

Chapter Twenty-three

It was time. Landon scrutinized his reflection in his bathroom mirror, as his heart served as the battlefield for a tug-of-war between fear and joy.

Landon exhaled. His consolation was Gina loved him. He grinned because he had professed his feelings first, but when Gina whispered those words back to him, he couldn't handle the overload of emotions he experienced hearing the admission from her lips the first time.

He expected the limousine to take him to Gina's house any minute. It was a cheezy way to propose, but it was too cold for a horse-drawn carriage ride.

This night would change his life forever. Ray Christmas had given his blessings. It was all about them. Landon locked his front door when the limo pulled to the curb in front of his house. Each step brought him closer to his heart's desire. Once in the backseat, Landon exhaled and fumbled with the envelope, which held more than the perfect Christmas card for Gina.

The festive decorations that hung from streetlight posts seemed to light his path throughout the city. Closing his eyes, Landon took deep breaths to calm his racing heart and quiet his jumbled thoughts. Tonight would be life-changing. Surreal.

He was about to propose to a woman he couldn't, wouldn't, and didn't want to live without. The moment was heavy, but the love in his heart was heavier as he prepared to take this leap of faith.

Soon, he arrived at Gina's. He got out and hiked the stairs to her front porch. She opened her door before he could reach the doorbell. The inside Christmas lights glowed behind her. For a moment, Landon wondered if his Granny Lonna had seen an angelic glow around Gina the first time she met her. His lady reminded him of one of the many angels he had seen on display at Christmas.

The long, metallic burgundy dress fell to her feet and exposed dark polished toes while a silver, furry wrap covered her shoulders.

One step, and he towered over Gina. Landon exhaled the cold air, which smelled like peppermint from his breath. "Ready?"

"Yes." Her voice was soft. She turned to lock her door, then fell into his waiting arms.

Could I love her anymore? He stared into her misty brown eyes. "Do I need a mistletoe to kiss the woman I love?"

"No." Gina closed her eyes and puckered her glossy lips.

Pulling her closer and tighter, Landon kissed Gina, then smiled at her dazed look when she opened her eyes.

"Come on. Our reservation is waiting." *And so is my heart.*

Gina felt like Cinderella, better than the make-believe times when she and Denise would dress as children and believe any popular teen idol was their prince.

Inside the limo, she snuggled next to Landon to enjoy pure bliss. A burgundy-and-brown tie complemented his brown suit. His shirt was crisp as if he'd just picked it up from the cleaners.

"Hey," Landon said, gently jostling her. "Are you going to sleep on me?"

Not opening her eyes, Gina shook her head, careful not to mess up her hairdo, which she had swept up on one side and held by a rhinestone pin. "I'm in a fairytale and don't want to open my eyes.

Landon chuckled. "You're going to have to tonight, baby, because I don't want you to miss a moment."

She did and noticed the driver leave the city limits. "Where are we going?"

"To a five-star restaurant," was all Landon would say.

Gina didn't care if he took her to White Castle for burgers and fries. They were together, dressed up, and she was very aware of his presence—from his heartbeat to his breathing. Gina mentally took notes so she would never forget tonight.

Soon, the driver stopped in the circular drive of Ballwin-Fritz Country Club.

The chauffeur opened the doors. Landon stepped out first, reached for her hand, and escorted her inside. They followed the host to a majestic ballroom where the ambiance was romantic with a live string quartet. He squeezed her hand. "Happy so far?"

Seriously? You didn't have to ask me. "Happy forever." Gina couldn't contain her happiness.

The food was pre-selected for the season, so there wasn't a menu for guests. Landon reached across the table and took both of her hands in his. She loved it when he did that. He brought them to his lips and brushed a kiss, tickling her with his silky trimmed mustache. His barber always did a great job.

"You know, there are some things we've never discussed."

Tilting her head, Gina studied him. "I can't imagine what that would be. We know a lot about each other's families, our faith walk with the Lord, favorite foods, colors, movies, music, giving to charities, and volunteering our time together."

"Even the quirky things, like my woman preferring to eat cold cereal at night instead of in the mornings."

"*Shh.*" She placed a finger to his lips. "That's my secret."

Landon chuckled. "There are no secrets between us, babe. Plus, you like the crunchy stuff, and I've heard more than once when we spoke over the phone at night."

"That's why I love you. I feel my vulnerability is safe with you. Coming to the children's home to help clean up, even though we hadn't been on the best terms, reminded me of the man you are. Then, when Leslie told me about a generous donation to the foundation and said your name, I knew it was because you trusted me."

"I don't ever want you to feel that I don't. We can disagree and not stop loving each other."

"I won't. Ever." Gina shook her head as her eyes watered.

Their plates were placed in front of them, and Landon gave thanks and asked for God's blessing. They flirted across the table while they savored their salmon and stuffed baked chicken.

This was a night to remember. When the dessert arrived, Landon stopped her before she could take the first bite.

"Here. I got you a card—a Christmas card." Landon pulled it from his suit jacket pocket and slid it across the table toward her.

Gina chuckled. "You already sent me a card." It was the most beautiful one on her mantel.

"Nope." He gave her a serious expression. "This is a special card that had to be hand delivered."

"Oh." Gina lifted a brow. Landon knew she collected beautifully designed or unique cards. Judging by the slight thickness of the red square envelope, it had to be a pop-up card.

His eyes began to sparkle like the gold dusting on the envelope. She carefully opened the seal and slipped out the card. A diamond ring fell out. She wanted to kneel and praise God for answering her prayer.

Instead, when she looked up, it was Landon who knelt.

"Gina Christmas, God gave me you as a gift, and it's almost Christmas. You are the best thing that has happened to me. Will you marry me so we can hold hands on life's journey and hug when we're having a bad day? Will you let me cook for you when you're sick in bed and love me until my last breath or the rapture, whichever comes first?"

Gina smiled as she placed her hands on both sides of his face and rested her forehead on his. "Yes, yes, yes."

Landon took the ring and slid it on her finger. It was a perfect fit, and so was their kiss.

Landon had been an engaged man to the most wonderful woman for two days. When she wasn't looking, he liked to watch Gina's expressions as she admired her diamond ring. What was she thinking? One question he didn't have to ask was whether she was happy. Landon could see it on her face and feel it in the air.

It was top secret to keep until Christmas Day when they would tell their families and showed them Gina's ring. It would be the best Christmas ever!

As they finished their last minute shopping for everyone's keepsakes, Gina received a surprise call from Leslie. She and Melody, from the children's home, put their heads together and tracked down the girl on social media who had created the Black angel Granny Lonna had purchased.

"Keisha Dobson was excited someone liked her work and was willing to create another angel for that customer…and she is going to personalize it to her," Leslie said.

Gina gave her the information to pass on to the artisan.

If the personalized ornament didn't make Granny Lonna happy, then Landon and Gina had done their best. Landon's engagement with Gina seemed to give his grandmother a new life.

"That's my Black angel," Granny Lonna hugged Gina and cried. When she saw the angel ornament, she smiled. "And you have you one." She patted Gina's arm. "I knew you would make a perfect match for my grandson when my husband and I visited your grandfather. You were a pretty little girl, playing with your doll. You have the most beautiful smile as a woman. I had hoped one day you and my grandson would meet. Before I knew there was a connection, I had purchased that ornament from Every Day is Christmas. When I heard you were also an accountant and on the board of the charity, I had hoped you and my Landon would meet." With every detail of her scheme, Granny Lonna proved her mind was as sharp as ever.

Landon and Gina stared at each other, then laughed. They had been set up.

Epilogue

Love had found Gina—finally! With a sigh of contentment, she turned in Landon's arms while they were in the middle of a New Year's Day movie marathon at his house. "A long or short engagement?" she teased.

"Fiancée, don't play with me." Landon tweaked her nose. "I'd marry you today if our mothers and Granny Lonna wouldn't have a fit."

Me too…sort of. Gina giggled. "True, but you know tax season kicks in at the end of the month, and—"

"And it's going to be painful for me." Landon groaned. "How much time do you need to plan?"

Lifting a brow, Gina twisted her mouth. "You mean *we*. Our mothers will help, but this is about our love, and no one else can express it better than we can."

Landon nodded. A slight pout flashed on his face.

"And any planning," Gina emphasized, "any planning during tax season is out. Christmas is a perfect time for a wedding."

"Arggh." He gritted his teeth in frustration. "Nine months tops, not twelve," he said repeatedly. "Lord, help me to hold out this long."

Gina rubbed his jaw. She understood. "We've made it this far, and God can keep us from falling because I don't want us to fall."

"Me either."

They were quiet as they held hands and looked at the ring.

"Just think, this wouldn't be possible without Denise's setup," Landon said. "And Granny Lonna, who, at the time, I thought was sending me on a wild goose chase."

Landon bit his bottom lip and grinned. "I can think of a good way to pay Denise back."

Gina perked up. "Really? How?"

"I've got people who might interest her. My best friend, Terrell, whom you've spoken to a few times, is a good guy and a brother to me. I've got two cousins, who I hope will be ready for a wife at our wedding."

"Were you looking?" Gina asked.

"No, but Christmas came early, and I got exactly what I wanted." He sealed it with a kiss.

About the Author

Pat Simmons is a multi-published Christian romance author of forty-plus titles. She is a self-proclaimed genealogy sleuth passionate about researching her ancestors and casting them in starring roles in her novels. She is a five-time recipient of the RSJ Emma Rodgers Award for Best Inspirational Romance: *Still Guilty, Crowning Glory, The Confession, Christmas Dinner*, and *Queen's Surrender (To A Higher Calling)*. Pat's first inspirational women's fiction, *Lean On Me*, with Sourcebooks, was the national library system's February/March Together We Read Digital Book Club pick. *Here for You* and *Stand by Me* are also part of the Family is Forever series. Her holiday indie release, *Christmas Dinner*, and traditionally published, *Here for You*, were featured in *Woman's World*, a national magazine. *Here for You* was also listed in the "7 Great Reads That Help to Keep the Faith" by Sisters From AARP. She contributed an article, "I'm Listening," in the *Chicken Soup for the Soul: I'm Speaking Now* (2021). Pat is the recipient of the 2022 Leslie Esdaile "Trailblazer" Award given by Building Relationships Around Books Readers' Choice for her work in the Christian fiction genre.

As a Christian, Pat describes the evidence of the gift of the Holy Ghost as a life-altering experience. She has been a featured speaker and workshop presenter at various venues nationwide. Pat has converted her sofa-strapped sports fanatical husband into an amateur travel agent, untrained bodyguard, GPS-guided chauffeur, and administrative assistant who is constantly on probation. They have a son and a daughter. Pat holds a B.S. in mass communications from Emerson College in Boston, Massachusetts, and has worked in radio, television, and print media for over twenty years. She oversaw the media publicity for the annual RT Booklovers Conventions for fourteen years. Visit her at www.patsimmons.net.

Other Christian Titles

The Jamieson Legacy
Book 1: Guilty of Love
Book 2: Not Guilty of Love
Book 3: Still Guilty
Book 4: The Acquittal
Book 5: Guilty by Association
Book 6: The Guilt Trip
Book 7: Free from Guilt
Book 8: Sandra Nicholson's Backstory
Book 9: The Confession
Book 10: The Guilty Generation
Book 11: Queen's Surrender (To a Higher Calling)
Book 12: Contempt: Grandma BB's Shenanigans
Book 13: Christmas Takeover (The Next Generation)
Book 14: Accomplices in Love (The Next Generation)

The Intercessors
Book 1: Day Not Promised
Book 2: Day She Prayed
Book 3: Days Are Coming
Book 4: Day of Salvation

The Carmen Sisters
Book 1: No Easy Catch
Book 2: In Defense of Love
Book 3: Driven to Be Loved
Book 4: Redeeming Heart

Love at the Crossroads
Book 1: Stopping Traffic
Book 2: A Baby for Christmas
Book 3: The Keepsake
Book 4: What God Has for Me
Book 5: Every Woman Needs a Praying Man

Restore My Soul
Book 1: Crowning Glory
Book 2: Jet: The Back Story
Book 3: Love Led by the Spirit

Family is Forever
Book 1: Lean on Me
Book 2: Here For You
Book 3: Stand by Me

Making Love Work Anthology
Book 1: Love at Work
Book 2: Words of Love
Book 3: A Mother's Love

God's Gifts
Book 1: Couple by Christmas
Book 2: Prayers Answered by Christmas

Perfect Chance at Love series
Book 1: Love by Delivery
Book 2: Late Summer Love

Single titles
Talk to Me
Her Dress
House Calls for the Holidays (short story)
Christmas Dinner
Christmas Greetings
Taye's Gift
Waiting for Christmas
House Calls for the Holidays
Anderson Brothers
Book 1: Love for the Holidays (Three novellas):
A Christian Christmas
A Christian Easter
A Christian Father's Day
Book 2: A Woman After David's Heart (A Valentine's Day Story)
Book 3: A Noelle for Nathan

In *Crowning Glory*, Cinderella had a prince; Karyn Wallace has a King. While Karyn served four years in prison for an unthinkable crime, she embraced salvation through the Crowns for Christ outreach ministry. After her release, Karyn stays strong and confident, despite society's stigma on ex-offenders. Since Christ strengthens the underdog, Karyn refuses to sway away from the scripture, "He whom the Son has set free is free indeed." Levi Tolliver, for the most part, is a practicing Christian. One contradiction is that he doesn't believe in turning the other cheek. He's steadfast that there is a price to pay for every sin committed, especially after the untimely death of his wife during a robbery. Then Karyn enters Levi's life. He is enthralled with her beauty and sweet spirit until he learns about her incarceration. If Levi can accept that Christ paid Karyn's debt in full, then a treasure awaits him. This is a powerful tale and reminds readers of the permanency of redemption.

Jet: The Back Story to Love Led By the Spirit, to say Jesetta "Jet" Hutchens issues is an understatement. In Crowning Glory, Book 1 of the Restoring My Soul series, she releases a firestorm of anger with an unforgiving heart. But every hurting soul has a history. In Jet: The

Back Story to Love Led by the Spirit, Jet doesn't know how to cope with losing her younger sister, Diane. But God sets her on the road to a spiritual recovery. To ensure she doesn't get lost, Jesus sends the handsome and single Minister Rossi Tolliver to guide her. Psalm 147:3 says Jesus can heal the brokenhearted and bind up their wounds. That sets the stage for Love Led by the Spirit.

In Love Led By the Spirit, Minister Rossi Tolliver is ready to settle down. Besides the outward attraction, he desires a sweet, humble woman who loves church folks. It sounds simple enough on paper, but when he gets off his knees, praying for that special someone to come into his life, God opens his eyes to the woman who has been there all along. There is only a slight problem. Love is the farthest thing from Jesetta "Jet" Hutchens' mind. But Rossi, the man, and the minister, is hard to resist. Is Jet ready to allow the Holy Spirit to lead her to love?

In *Stopping Traffic*, Book 1, Candace Clark has a phobia about crossing the street, and for a good reason. As fate would have it, her daughter's principal assigns her to crossing guard duties as part of the school's Parent Participation program. With no choice in the matter, Candace begrudgingly accepts her stop sign and safety vest, then reports to her designated crosswalk. Once Candace is determined to overcome her fears, God opens the door for a blessing, and Royce Kavanaugh enters her life, a firefighter built to rescue any damsel in distress. When a spark of attraction ignites, Candace and Royce soon discover more than one way to stop traffic.

In *A Baby For Christmas*, Book 2, yes, diamonds are a girl's best friend, but in Solae Wyatt-Palmer's case, she desires something more valuable. Captain Hershel Kavanaugh is a divorcee and the father of two adorable little boys. Solae has never been married and longs to be a mother. Although Hershel showers her with expensive gifts, his hesitation about proposing causes Solae to walk and never look back. As the holidays approach, Hershel must convince Solae she has everything he could ever want for Christmas.

In *The Keepsake*, Book 3, Until death us do part…or until Desiree walks away. Desiree "Desi" Bishop is devastated when she finds evidence of her husband's affair. God knew she didn't get married only to one day have to stand before a judge and file for a divorce. But Desi wants out no matter how much her heart says to forgive Michael. That isn't easier said than done. She sees God's one acceptable reason for a divorce as the only opt-out clause in her marriage. Michael Bishop is a repenting man who loves his wife of three years. If only…he had paid attention to the red flags God sent to keep him from falling into the devil's snares. But Michael didn't and fell. Although God forgives him instantly when he repents, Desi's forgiveness is moving as a snail's pace. In the end, after all the tears have been shed and forgiveness granted and received, the couple learns that some marriages are worth keeping.

In *What God Has For Me*, Book 4, pregnant or not, Halcyon Holland is leaving her boyfriend. When her ex makes no attempts to reconcile their relationship, Halcyon begins to second-guess whether or not she compromised her chance for a happily ever after. But Zachary Bishop has had his eye on Halcyon since he first saw her. What one man doesn't cherish, Zach is ready to treasure. He's on a mission to offer her a second chance at love that she can't refuse: unconditional love for a ready-made family. Halcyon will soon learn that her past circumstances won't hinder the Lord's blessings for them.

In *Every Woman Needs A Praying Man*, Book 5, first impressions can make or break a business deal, and they definitely could be a relationship buster, but an ill-timed panic attack draws two strangers together. Unlike firefighters who run into danger, instincts tell businessman Tyson Graham to be weary of a certain damsel in distress and run. Days later, the same woman struts through his door for a job interview. Monica Wyatt might possess the outward beauty and the brains on paper, but Tyson doesn't trust her to work for his firm, or maybe he doesn't trust his heart around her.

In *Guilty of Love*, when do you know the most important decision of your life is the right one? Reaping the seeds from what she's sown; Cheney Reynolds moves into a historic neighborhood in Ferguson, Missouri, and becomes a reclusive. Her first neighbor, the incomparable Mrs. Beatrice Tilley Beacon aka Grandma BB, is an opinionated childless widow. Grandma BB is a self-proclaimed expert on topics Cheney isn't seeking advice—everything from landscaping to hip-hop dancing to romance. Then there is Parke Kokumuo Jamison VI, a direct descendant of a royal African tribe. He learned his family ancestry, African history, and lineage preservation before he could count. Unwittingly, they are drawn to each other, but it takes Christ to weave their lives into a spiritual bliss while He exonerates their past indiscretions.

In *Not Guilty*, one man, one woman, one God, and one big problem. Malcolm Jamieson wasn't the man who got away, but the man God instructed Hallison Dinkins to set free. Instead of their explosive love affair leading them to the wedding altar, God diverted Hallison to the prayer altar during her first visit back to church in years.

Malcolm was convinced that his woman had loss her mind to break off their engagement. Didn't Hallison know that Malcolm, a tenth-generation descendant of a royal African tribe, couldn't be replaced? Once Malcolm concedes that their relationship can't be savaged, he issues Hallison his own edict, "If we're meant to be with each other, we'll find our way back. If not, that means there's a love stronger than we had." His words begin to haunt Hallison until she begins to regret their break up, and that's where their story begins. Someone has to retreat, and God never loses a battle.

In *Still Guilty*, Cheney Reynolds Jamieson made a choice years ago that is now shaping her future and the future of the men she loves. A botched abortion prevented her from carrying a baby to term, and her husband, Parke K. Jamison VI, is expected to produce heirs. With a wife who cannot give him a child, Parke vows to find and get custody of his illegitimate son by any means necessary. Meanwhile, Cheney's twin brother, Rainey, struggles with his anger over his ex-girlfriend's actions that haunt him, and their father, Dr. Roland Reynolds, fights to keep an old secret in the past.

In *The Acquittal*, two worlds apart, but their hearts dance to the same African drum beat. On a professional level, Dr. Rainey Reynolds is a competent, highly sought-after orthodontist. Inwardly, he needs to be set free from the chaos of revelations that make him question if happiness is obtainable. To get away from the drama, Rainey is willing to leave the country under the guise of a mission trip with Dentist Without Borders. Will changing his surroundings really change him? If one woman can heal his wounds, then he will believe that there is really peace after the storm.

Ghanaian beauty Josephine Abena Yaa Amoah returns to Africa after completing her studies as an exchange student in St. Louis, Missouri. Although her heart bleeds for his peace, she knows she must step back and pray for Rainey's surrender to Christ so God can acquit him of his self-inflicted mental torture. In the Motherland of Ghana, Africa, Rainey not only visits the places of his ancestors, will he embrace the liberty that Christ's Blood does set every man free.

In *Guilty By Association*, how important is a name? To the St. Louis Jamiesons, tenth-generation descendants of a royal African tribe—everything. To the Boston Jamiesons whose father never married their mother—there is no loyalty or legacy. Kidd Jamieson suffers from the "angry" male syndrome because his father was absent in the home, but insisted his two sons carry his last name. It takes an old woman who mingles genealogy truths and Bible verses together for Kidd to realize his worth as a strong black man. He learns it's not his association with the name that identifies him, but the man he becomes that defines him.

In *The Guilt Trip*, Aaron "Ace" Jamieson lives carefree. He's good-looking, and respectable when he's in the mood, but his weakness is women. If a woman tries to ambush him with a pregnancy, he takes off in the other direction. It's a lesson learned from his absentee father that responsibility is optional. Talise Rogers has a bright future ahead of her. She's pretty and has no problem catching a man's eye, which is exactly what she does with Ace. Trapping Ace Jamieson is the furthest thing from Talise's mind when she learns she is pregnant and Ace rejects her. "I want nothing from you Ace, not even your name." And Talise meant it.

In *Free From Guilt*, it's salvation round-up time and Cameron Jamieson's name is on God's hit list. Although his brothers and cousins embraced God—thanks to the women in their lives—the two-degreed MIT graduate isn't going to let any woman take him down that path without a fight. He's satisfied with his career, social calendar, and good genes. But God uses a beautiful messenger, Gabrielle Dupree, to show him that he's in a spiritual deficit. Cameron learns the hard way that man's wisdom is like foolishness to God. For every philosophical argument he throws her way, Gabrielle exposes him to scriptures that makes him question his worldly knowledge.

In *Sandra Nicholson's Backstory*, Sandra has made good and bad choices throughout the years, but the best one was to give her life to Christ when her sons were small and to rear them up in the best Christian way she knew how. That was thirty-something years ago and Sandra has evolved from a young single mother of two rambunctious boys: Kidd and Ace Jamieson, to a godly woman seasoned with wisdom. Despite the challenges and trials of rearing two strong-willed personalities, Sandra maintained her sanity through the grace of God, which kept gray strands at bay. But there is something to be said about a woman's first love. Kidd and Ace Jamieson's father, Samuel Jamieson broke their mother's heart. Can Sandra recover? Her sons don't believe any man is good enough for her, especially their absent father. Kidd doesn't deny his mother should find love again since she never married Samuel. But will she fall for a carbon copy of his father? God's love gives second chances.

In *The Confession*, Sandra Nicholson had made good and bad choices throughout the years, but the best one was to give her life to Christ when her sons were small and to rear them up in the best Christian way she knew how. That was thirty-something years ago and Sandra has evolved from a young single mother of two rambunctious boys, Kidd and Ace Jamieson to a godly woman seasoned with wisdom. Despite the challenges and trials of rearing two strong-willed personalities, Sandra maintained her sanity through the grace of God, which kept gray strands at bay.

Now, Sandra Nicholson is on the threshold of happiness, but Kidd believes no man is good enough for his mother, especially if her love interest could be a man just like his absentee father.

In *The Guilty Generation*, seventeen-year-old Kami Jamieson is so over being daddy's little girl. Now that she has captured the attention of Tango, the bad boy from her school, Kami's love for her family and God have taken a backseat to her teen crush. Although the Jamiesons have instilled godly principles in Kami since she was young, they will stop at nothing, including prayer and fasting, to protect her from falling prey to society's peer pressure. Can Kami survive her teen rebellion, or will she be guilty of dividing the next generation?

In *Queen's Surrender (To a Higher Calling)*, Opposites attract...or clash. The Jamieson saga continues with the Queen of the family in this inspirational romance. She's the mistress of flirtation but Philip is unaffected by her charm. The two enjoy a harmless banter about God's will versus Queen's, who prefers her own free-will lifestyle. Philip doesn't judge her choices—most of the time—and Queen respects his opinions—most of the time. It's perfect harmony sometimes. Queen, the youngest sister of the Jamieson clan, wears her name as if it's a crown. She's single, sassy, and most of the time, loving her status, but she's about to strut down an unexpected spiritual path. Evangelist Philip Dupree is on the hot seat as the trial pastor at Total Surrender Church. The stalemate: They want a family man to lead their flock. The board's ultimatum is enough to make him quit the ministry. But can a man of God walk away from his calling? Can two people with different lifestyles and priorities cross paths and continue the journey as one? Who is going to be the first to surrender?

In *Contempt (Grandma BB's Shenanigans)*, Grandma BB, the unofficial matriarch of the Jamieson clan, is getting her house in order for the perfect homegoing celebration. After all, she's eighty-something. She summons Parke Jamieson VI, his brothers, cousins, and their families to play a part in the practice funeral program—only if they follow her instructions to the letter. Since the Jamiesons are at her house with bodyguards Chip and Dale, they might have an impromptu family game night. The evening is full of surprises, especially when an unexpected visitor shows up to steal the show. With more work that needs to be done, Grandma BB plans to put her funeral on hold and stick around for a couple more generations.

In *Accomplices in Love*, Parke "Pace" Jamieson VIII knows something is special about Harmony Reed, his sister's college friend who was almost stranded in St. Louis for Christmas. She checks all his compatibility boxes: looks, charm, a great sense of humor, and strong attraction. Plus, the Jamiesons love her.

When not at school, Harmony lives in Chicago with her three overprotective brothers. She is not interested in a relationship with her best friend's brother.

Pace, who lives in St. Louis, is not deterred by the distance, her objections, or her brothers. He's a Jamieson, and they play to win.

In *Fun and Games with the Jamieson Men*, The Jamieson Legacy series inspired this game book of fun activities:• Brain Teasers• Crossword Puzzles• Word Searches •Sudoku •Mazes •Coloring Pages. The Jamiesons are fictional characters that put emphasis on Black Heritage, which includes Black American History tidbits, African American genealogy, and strong Black families. Relax, grab a pencil and play along.

THE CARMEN SISTERS SERIES

In *No Easy Catch*, Book 1, Shae Carmen hasn't lost her faith in God, only the men she's come across. Shae's recent heartbreak was discovering that her boyfriend was not only married, but on the verge of reconciling with his estranged wife. Humiliated, Shae begins to second guess herself as why she didn't see the signs that he was nothing more than a devil's decoy masquerading as a devout Christian man. St. Louis Outfielder Rahn Maxwell finds himself a victim of an attempted carjacking. The Lord guides him out of harms' way by opening the gunmen's eyes to Rahn's identity. The crook instead becomes an infatuated fan and asks for Rahn's autograph, and as a goodwill gesture, directs Rahn out of the ambush! When the news media gets wind of what happened with the baseball player, Shae's television station lands an exclusive interview. Shae and Rahn's chance meeting sets in motion a relationship where Rahn not only surrenders to Christ, but pursues Shae with a purpose to prove that good men are still out there. After letting her guard down, Shae is faced with another scandal that rocks her world. This time the stakes are higher. Not only is her heart on the line, so is her professional credibility. She and Rahn are at odds as how to handle it and friction erupts between them. Will she strike out at love again? The Lord shows Rahn that nothing happens by chance, and everything is done for Him to get the glory.

In *Defense of Love*, Book 2, nothing in Garrett Nash's life has made sense lately. When two people close to the U.S. Marshal wrong him deeply, Garrett expects God to remove them from his life. Instead, the Lord relocates Garrett to another city to start over, as if he were the offender instead of the victim. Criminal attorney Shari Carmen is comfortable in her own skin—most of the time. Being a "dark and lovely" African-American sister has its challenges, especially when it comes to relationships. Although she's a fireball in the courtroom, she knows how to fade into the background and keep the proverbial spotlight off her personal life. But literal spotlights are a different matter altogether. While playing tenor saxophone at an anniversary party, she grabs the attention of Garrett Nash. And as God draws them closer together, He makes another request of Garrett, one to which it will prove far more difficult to say "Yes, Lord."

In *Redeeming Heart*, Book 3, Landon Thomas (In Defense of Love) brings a new definition to the word "prodigal," as in prodigal son, brother or anything else imaginable. It's good that God's love covers a multitude of sins, but He isn't letting Landon off easy. His journey from riches to rags proves to be humbling and a lesson well learned. Real Estate Agent Octavia Winston is a woman on a mission, whether it's God's or hers professionally. One thing is for certain, she's not about to compromise when it comes to a Christian mate, so why did God send a homeless man to steal her heart? Minister Rossi Tolliver (Crowning Glory) knows how to minister to God's lost sheep and through God's redemption, the game changes for Landon and Octavia.

In *Driven to Be Loved*, Book 4, on the surface, Brecee Carmen has nothing in common with Adrian Cole. She is a pediatrician certified in trauma care; he is a transportation problem solver for a luxury car dealership (a.k.a., a car salesman). Despite their slow but steady attraction to each other, neither one of them are sure that they're compatible. To complicate matters, Brecee is the sole unattached Carmen when it seems as though everyone else around her—family and friends—are finding love, except her. Through a series of discoveries, Adrian and Brecee learn that things don't happen by coincidence. Generational forces are at work, keeping promises, protecting family members, and perhaps even drawing Adrian back to the church. For Brecee and Adrian, God has been hard at work, playing matchmaker all along the way for their paths cross at the right time and the right place.

Lean on Me, Book 1. No one should have to go it alone... Caregivers sometimes need a little TLC too.

Tabitha Knicely believes in family before everything. She may be overwhelmed caring for her beloved great-aunt, but she would never turn her back on the woman who raised her, even if Aunt Tweet's dementia is getting worse. Tabitha is sure she can do this on her own. But when Aunt Tweet ends up on her neighbor's front porch, and the man has the audacity to accuse Tabitha of elder abuse, things go from bad to awful. Marcus Whittington feels a mountain of regret at causing problems for Tabitha and her great-aunt. How was he to know the frail older woman's niece was doing the best she could? As Marcus gets to know Aunt Tweet and sees how hard Tabitha is fighting to keep everything together, he can't walk away from the pair. Particularly when helping Tabitha care for her great-aunt leads the two of them on a spiritual journey of faith and surrender.

Here For You, Book 2. Rachel Knicely's life has been on hold for six months while she takes care of her great aunt, who has Alzheimer's. Putting her aunt first was an easy decision—accepting that Aunt Tweet is nearing the end of her battle is far more difficult. Nicholas Adams's ministry is bringing comfort to those who are sick and homebound. He responds to a request for help for an ailing woman but when he meets the Knicelys, he realizes Rachel is the one who needs support the most. Nicholas is charmed by and attracted to Rachel, but then devastating news brings both a crisis of faith and roadblocks to their budding relationship that neither could have anticipated. This beautifully emotional and clean story contains a hero and heroine who are better at taking care of other people than themselves, a dark moment that shakes their faith, and a well-earned happily ever after.

Stand by Me, Book 3. An uplifting story about embracing love and giving others—and yourself—one more chance. When it comes to being a caregiver, Kym Knicely has been there and done that. Then she meets Charles "Chaz" Banks and soon learns that every caregiving situation is different. Chaz takes care of his seven-year-old autistic granddaughter, Chauncy. Although Kym's attraction to Chaz is strong, she has to decide whether a romantic relationship can survive and thrive between two people at different stages in life. It's a journey with a different set of rules that Kym has to play by if she and Chaz are to have their happily ever after and the faith and family they envision.

About *Waiting for Christmas*,

A chance meeting. An undeniable attraction.

And a first date that starts with a stakeout that leads to a winner takes all shopping spree. It's the making of a holiday romance. While philanthropist Sterling Price believes in charitable causes, he and licensed social worker Ciara Summers have a difference of opinion on how to bless others. Ciara is a rebel with a cause and a hundred reasons why helping those less fortunate is important. Sterling is a man of means who believes there is a financial responsibility that comes with giving.

The Lord will make sure everyone's needs are met, and He has something extra for Sterling and Ciara that can't wait until Christmas.

About *Christmas Dinner*,

How do you celebrate the holidays after losing a loved one? Take the journey, beginning with Christmas Dinner. For months, Darcelle Price has suffered depression in silence. But things are about to change as she plans to celebrate Christmas Eve with family and share her journey. Darcelle invites them via group text, not knowing she had included her ex. Evanston Giles is surprised to hear from the woman he loved after months following their breakup. Seeking closure, he shows up on her doorstep for answers. A lot can happen on Christmas Eve. Restoring family ties, building her faith in God, and falling in love again is just the beginning of the night of miracles.

About *Taye's Gift*,

Welcome to Snowflake, Colorado—a small town where wishes come true! When six old high school friends receive a letter that their fellow friend, Charity Hart, wrote before she passed away, their lives take an unexpected turn. She leaves them each a check for $1,500 and asks them to grant a wish—a secret wish—for someone else by Christmas. Who lays off someone before the holidays? Taye Thomas' employer did, so instead of Christmas shopping, she's job hunting. More devastating news comes when an old high school friend passed away. Could God be answering her prayers for help when she learns that Charity Hart left a $1500 check? No, the caveat is it's more blessed to give than receive. Taye has 30 days to find someone else in need to bless. To complicate matters, she's lives in Kansas City, which is more than eight hours away from Snowflake and she can't do it alone. Keeping a secret has never been so much work.

About *Couple by Christmas*,

Holidays haven't been the same for Derek Washington since his divorce. He and his ex-wife, Robyn, go out of their way to avoid each other. This Christmas may be different when he decides to give his son, Tyler, the family he once had before they split. Derek's going to need the Lord's intervention to soften her heart to agree to some outings. God's help doesn't come in the way he expected, but it's all good because everything falls in place for them to be a couple by Christmas.

About *Prayers Answered By Christmas*,

Christmas is coming. While other children are compiling their lists for a fictional Santa, eight-year-old Mikaela Washington is on her knees, making her requests known to the Lord: One mommy for Christmas please. Portia Hunter refuses to let her ex-husband cheat her out of the family she wants. Her prayer is for God to send the right man into her life. Marlon Washington will do anything for his two little girls, but can he find a mommy for them and a love for himself? Since Christmas is the time of year to remember the many gifts God has given men, maybe these three souls will get their heart s desire.

About *A Noelle for Nathan*,

A Noelle for Nathan is a story of kindness, selflessness, and falling in love during the Christmas season. Andersen Investors & Consultants, LLC, CFO Nathan Andersen (A Christian Christmas) isn't looking for attention when he buys a homeless man a meal, but grade school teacher Noelle Foster is watching his every move with admiration. His generosity makes him a man after her own heart. While donors give more to children and families in need around the holiday season, Noelle Foster believes in giving year-round after seeing many of her students struggle with hunger and finding a warm bed at night. At a second-chance meeting, sparks fly when Noelle and Nathan share a kindred spirit with their passion to help those less fortunate. Whether they're doing charity work or attending Christmas parties, the couple becomes inseparable. Although Noelle and Nathan exchange gifts, the biggest present is the one from Christ.

One reader says, "A Noelle for Nathan makes you fall in love with love…the love of mankind and the love of God. You cannot read this without having a desire to give and do more, all while being appreciative of what you have."

About *Christmas Greetings*,

Saige Carter loves everything about Christmas: the shopping, the food, the lights, and of course, Christmas wouldn't be complete without family and friends to share in the traditions they've created together. Plus, Saige is extra excited about her line of Christmas greeting cards hitting store shelves, but when she gets devastating news around the holidays, she wonders if she'll ever look at Christmas the same again. Daniel Washington is no Scrooge, but he'd rather skip the holidays altogether than spend them with his estranged family. After one too many arguments around the dinner table one year, Daniel had enough and walked away from the drama. As one year has turned into many, no one seems willing to take the first step toward reconciliation. When Daniel reads one of Saige's greeting cards, he's unsure if the words inside are enough to erase the pain and bring about forgiveness. Once God reveals His purpose for their lives to them, they will have a reason to rejoice. Come unto me, all ye that labor and are heavily laden, and I will give you rest. Take my yoke upon you, and learn of me; for I am meek and lowly in heart: and ye shall find rest unto your souls. Matthew 11:28-29

About *A Baby for Christmas*,

Yes, diamonds are a girl's best friend, but unless the jewel is going on Solae Wyatt-Palmer's ring finger, they hold little value to her. When she meets Fire Captain Hershel Kavanaugh, their magnetism is undeniable and there's no doubt that it's love at first sight. Since Solae adores Hershel's two boys from his failed marriage, she wouldn't blink at the chance to become a mother to them. But when it seems as if Hershel doesn't have a proposal on his agenda, she has no choice but to cut her losses and move on. But Christmas is coming. And in order to win Solae back, Hershel must resolve some past issues before convincing her that she possesses everything he wants.

About *A Christian Christmas*,

Christmas will never be the same for Joy Knight if Christian Andersen has his way. Not to be confused with a secret Santa, Christian and his family are busier than Santa's elves making sure the Lord's blessings are distributed to those less fortunate by Christmas day. Joy is playing the hand that life dealt her, rearing four children in a home that is on the brink of foreclosure. She's not looking for a handout, but when Christian rescues her in the checkout line; her niece thinks Christian is an angel. Joy thinks he's just another man who will eventually leave, disappointing her and the children. Although Christian is a servant of the Lord, he is a flesh and blood man and all he wants for Christmas is Joy Knight. Can time spent with Christian turn Joy's attention from her financial woes to the real meaning of Christmas—and true love? A Christian Christmas is a holiday novella to be enjoyed any time of the year.

In *Every Day is Christmas*,

A Christmas ornament, an ailing grandmother, and a match-making sister are all ingredients for a holiday romance.

Landon Michaels is on a mission to fulfill this grandmother's request for a one-of-a-kind Black angel ornament. With dementia setting in, this might be the last Christmas she remembers.

Gina Christmas is the gatekeeper of unique handcrafted ornaments. It's tax season, and the accountant is too busy crunching numbers to track down an ornament, especially since the holiday is months away.

When Granny Lonna wants something, Landon, her favorite and only grandson, is determined to make it happen. But what she really wants for Christmas is for Landon to find the perfect love.

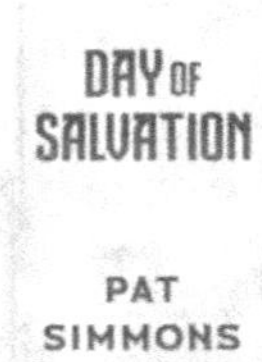

The Intercessors

Pat Simmons introduces a new Christian fiction series that reminds readers that the bad guys don't always win, especially when the Lord fights our battles.

In *Day Not Promised*, Omega Addams thought it was a typical workday until a detour on the way home changes everything. She's almost killed, but an innocent bystander, Mitchell Franklin, takes a bullet for Omega during a gas station robbery. In the aftermath, Omega has no idea that God expects her to "pray it forward" until a spiritual battle unfolds before her eyes. Another innocent bystander is in trouble; unless Omega gets her prayer life together, others will die without Christ. It's a chain reaction that highlights the responsibility of a Christian-- hot, cold, or lukewarm. It's time to get our acts together. We are our brother's keeper.

In *Day She Prayed*, New Christian convert Tally Gilbert knows the power of prayer and the pain of walking away. She's witnessed family and friends' healing, salvation, and deliverance. There's one holdout, and he's at the top of her prayer list. The love of her life, Randall Addams, won't surrender to the Lord, so Tally ends the relationship. What will it take for Randall to turn to God?

Will Tally's prayers be answered, or will Randall—and their love—be lost forever?

Don't underestimate a woman who knows how to pray, has backup, and believes "The Word of God is quick, and powerful, and sharper than any two-edged sword, piercing even to the dividing the soul from the spirit, and of the joints and marrow, and is a discerner of the thoughts and intents of the heart." Hebrews 4:12.

If the devil wants a battle, he picks the wrong woman to fight.

In *Days Are Coming, I'm coming for the children.*

Minister Jude Morgan has a strong relationship with the Lord but doesn't know what the latest message means. He is determined to intercede for his young mentee, Carlton Oliver, and children worldwide.

Nine-year-old Carlton wants to get to know his estranged dad, but at what cost? He's about to discover many things he doesn't know about the man who fathered him, and he's on a mission to worship the Lord.

Sinclaire Oliver regrets getting her ex, Harrison Wakefield, involved in her life and that of his son Carlton. He's more trouble than the monthly child support payments she had to sue for. She knows he's angry but never expects it to take a dark turn. Sinclaire learns that God makes no mistakes, even when things don't make sense.

As God sends His judgment on the earth, the devil plants decoys to distract the saints from their mission to be on guard. Is the world doomed, or is there room for redemption?

In *Day of Salvation*, Mother Kincaid, from Christ Is For All Church, has been fervently praying, along with other prayer warriors around the world, for Jesus to return and rescue His saints from this wicked world.

One day, God answers her with a list of unknown individuals who need salvation and a commission for the intercessors and prayer warriors to find and draw them to Christ. Then He will come to redeem His saints, and judgment will begin on the earth.

The caveat to the Lord God's edict: the timer has been set, and if the intercessors don't witness to them, those people will be lost forever.

God thunders, "Get set, get ready, GO!!!!!"